The Ranger Shield Security Series

BETRAYAL & NEW BEGINNINGS

INSTINCT & NEW IDENTITY

DECEPTION & NEW DIRECTION

RESTART & NEW REVENGE

For more information visit www.AllisonBettes.com.

Betrayal

AND NEW

BEGINNINGS

A RANGER SHIELD SECURITY NOVEL

ALLISON BETTES

This is a work of fiction created without use of AI technology. Any names, characters, businesses, places, events, and incidents portrayed in this novel are either products of the author's imagination or are used fictitiously. Any resemblance to actual persons, living or dead, places, or events is purely coincidental or fictional.

www.allisonbettes.com

Betrayal

AND NEW

BEGINNINGS

A RANGER SHIELD SECURITY NOVEL

CONTENT WARNING

This book contains themes and discussions related to domestic abuse, including emotional and physical violence. While these elements are essential to the story, they may be distressing for some readers. Please proceed with care and remember to prioritize your well-being.

If you or someone you know is experiencing domestic abuse, help is available. In the U.S., you can reach the National Domestic Violence Hotline at 800-799-7233 or visit www.thehotline.org for resources and support.

To my husband, Mike, and my best friend Haley, for giving me the confidence I needed to publish these books.

To my amazing author friends, Jocelyn Fox and Susan Hendricks—thank you both for answering the 7,391 questions I had about this process.

To my editors, Jenny, Sherri, and Monica, and my beta readers Leah and Sara—thank you for helping me bring this book to life.

Finally, to Kristen Ashley, one of my favorite authors of all time—you don't know me, but your documents on self-publishing became my bible for months. Thank you for unknowingly helping me become a published author.

PROLOGUE
ELLIE

Deep breaths. If you're feeling this much pain, it means you're alive. Now you need to stay alive.

As the world spun around me, I reminded myself to just keep taking deep breaths.

Everything hurt. Every part of my body, from my head to my feet. Memories began to flood my mind as I tried to open my eyes.

Randall had slapped me, punched me, and threw me against a wall. He yelled obscene things about how awful I was and how I deserved this.

I thought of my brother, Jack, who would be so disappointed in me. He'd hated Randall from the very beginning and had told me to break up with him.

"Ellie-girl, that dude is bad news. Stay the hell away from him," Jack, always blunt, had said to me.

But like the strong-willed, stubborn woman I was, I'd

wanted to prove to Jack that I could make my own decisions, and he didn't have to take care of me anymore.

All I could think about right now as I lay here in so much pain was that my brother was right about Randall, and I wish I had listened to him.

"What's this?" Randall startled me as I put clothes in my suitcase. I didn't hear him come home because I was so focused on getting packed as quickly as possible.

"Why are you packing a bag? Are you fucking leaving me?" he yelled and stepped closer to me.

I tried to scoot back, but there was no place to escape. The door to the bedroom was blocked and the window was on the other side. Not that I would be able to open it and jump out before he got me anyway.

He wasn't supposed to come home from work for at least another two hours. I knew his schedule and he never came home early on Thursdays. Ever. Many times, he even went out with friends after work for a few drinks. I thought today was safe.

My friend Katie was on her way to help me pack and get out of there. I needed to find a way to calm him down and leave before she got here, or he would hurt her, too.

"I asked you a question, Elliana! Why are you packing your bags?" he screamed and moved even closer.

"I wa-was going to go visit my brother. He's, uh, getting his leave a few weeks early," I tried to say with as much muster as I could, knowing it was a complete lie.

"Bullshit! You don't need this much stuff to visit him for a couple of days," he said as he came within inches of my

face. "You are mine, Elliana Hutchinson!" he yelled as he slapped me hard across the face. "You will never leave me. Do you understand?"

His hands wrapped around my neck as he squeezed and yelled. I tried gasping for air but couldn't get any. The next punch was all I remembered and then the world went black.

As I drove to my fresh start in Georgia, I let my mind wander to several days ago, when my life came crashing down around me.

Thankfully, Katie had pulled up to the house just as Randall was leaving in his car. Knowing he wasn't supposed to be there, she'd waited, then came to the front door and knocked. When I repeatedly hadn't answered she'd known something was wrong. I had given her a key in case of emergency, so she'd let herself in and found me bloodied on the floor. I'd awoken quickly after she got there and told her I didn't want to go to the hospital because it would only make escaping more difficult.

To avoid the risk of Randall breaking into my car that had been left on his driveway, Katie had moved my car two blocks away from his house right after she picked me up. It was meant to be a temporary fix while I stayed with her.

Katie was staying with her parents in order to save money and help pay off her student loans, and thankfully they were away on a trip. She'd taken me back to their place to get cleaned up, and since she was almost done with nursing school, she'd watched me all night to check for signs of a concussion.

I'd stayed with her for five days until I'd felt healed enough to leave. I hadn't been lying when I'd told Randall I was going to Georgia to visit Jack. It was just that Jack wasn't going to be there, at least not right away.

Once I'd made the decision to leave Randall, I'd messaged Jack to let him know I had quit my job as a waitress and bartender and was moving to Georgia to be closer to him. His reply email had been short, but he'd seemed genuinely happy, especially about me leaving Randall. He'd said his last tour was almost done, but not for a few more weeks, so I should just stay at his place until he got home and then he would help me find my own apartment.

He'd also mentioned his buddy and former sergeant owned the pub below his apartment, so he would check with him about getting me a job there. I hated getting handouts, but I didn't really have a choice since I was moving to a new city and didn't know anybody there.

My parents had died in a car crash when I was thirteen and Jack was eighteen. We went to live with our grandma, but only four months later, Jack graduated and enlisted in the Army. I loved my brother, but it had felt like another family member had been ripped away from me. We'd written to each other all the time while he was deployed and spent most of his trips home together with Gran in Tennessee, where she raised us in the house our mom grew up in, but it always irked me when Jack tried to intervene in my life when he had no problem walking away to begin with. I now understand why he did, though, because Gran was retired and living off what little money our parents left behind, so Jack had felt he had to enlist so he could send money back to Gran to help raise me.

So here I was, on the road, and had finally crossed into Georgia. "Road to freedom," Katie had called it, but it certainly didn't feel like it. Not yet, at least. My plan was to head straight to the pub and meet his buddy Wade to get the spare key to my brother's apartment and hopefully interview for a job. Maybe this next phase of my life would go a little smoother.

1

WADE

The lunch rush at the restaurant had just ended, leaving us in the usual lull before the dinner crowd arrived. The Watering Hole, the pub I co-owned with my friends—most of whom were former military, along with one former cop—wasn't exactly where I envisioned my career heading. Still, it was part of our larger plan after retiring from the military. Vince, Jack, and I had served together during my last tour, and during downtime, we often talked about our post-duty ambitions. Vince's cousin, a cop looking to transition into private security, inspired us to team up with him and Archer to bring our vision to life.

Considering three of us were Army Rangers, our special ops skills made us highly qualified to do private security. Vince, having learned from his bounty hunter dad, and Archer, a former cop, also allowed us to add private investigations and fugitive recovery to our business.

However, a business like that usually takes time to build up clientele, so we'd decided to buy into the pub first to build up cash flow for the security business. My uncle ran the Watering Hole for thirty years, but was ready to retire, so I'd talked him into selling the pub and restaurant to me. The best part was he owned the whole building. The pub was on the ground floor, with a large empty space on the second floor, which we'd turned into the security company, and then two small apartments on the floor above that.

I lived in one apartment, and the other belonged to Jack, though I mainly kept an eye on it now while he was finishing up his last tour. Once he was done, hopefully in a few weeks, he would join us at the security company.

We'd recently put in a surveillance room upstairs where we could monitor all the extra security cameras we installed around the inside and outside of the building. It was necessary for the security company, but also for the pub, so I could keep an eye on everything when I wasn't there.

It was a great location, just on the north side of Atlanta near Dobbington Air Reserve Base. Plenty of servicemembers came to the bar during downtime, which made it a good spot to recruit more people for when our business - Ranger Shield Security - took off. Archer and Vince were basically heading up the security company since Jack was still overseas, and I was running the bar most days.

Jack had called a couple of days ago to give me a

heads-up that his sister was going to move into his space temporarily until he came home. He didn't say much, but apparently his sister quit her job, broke up with her boyfriend and was moving here. He also asked if we could hire her at the bar, which was fine by me because we were short-staffed, and she apparently had experience working in restaurants and bars. He gave her my cell, and she'd texted me to tell me she would be here this afternoon, which was what I was currently waiting for.

I was hoping to get her to fill out all the paperwork and give her the basics today and then have her start training tomorrow with Tammy, who had been here about as long as my uncle. Speak of the feisty devil, Tammy stood in the small office doorway and knocked.

"Hey boss-man, got a lady here to see ya. A real looker named Ellie. Is this the one you want me training?"

"Yeah. Would you send her back so we can get started on her paperwork?"

"Sure thing. I'm glad we share tips, 'cause I have a feelin' this one will bring in lots of them from the boys. She's certainly easier on the eyes than Sam and Corey," Tammy said with a wink.

"Thanks, Tammy," I said as I rolled my eyes. Tammy had made it her life's mission lately to try setting me up with every girl who walked into the bar, no matter how big the red flags were.

Small raps at the door had me looking up again, and I immediately did a double-take of the woman standing next to Tammy. She hadn't been kidding. This woman was stunning. Jack had a picture of him and his sister he carried around with him while we were overseas, but the girl in the picture was a scrawny fourteen-year-old girl with frizzy blond hair and braces. The woman before me was not that girl. She had filled out in all the right places.

She was quite tall. She practically towered over Tammy, though that wasn't saying much since almost everyone was taller than Tammy, but what Tammy lacked in height, she more than made up for with attitude and brass balls.

"Here ya go, boss. Once y'all get the paperwork signed let me know, and I can show her around the place and figure out a time for her to shadow me."

"Thanks Tammy. Will do," I said, shaking myself out of my daze as I stared at the beautiful woman in the doorway. I noticed some discoloration on her face – bruises, maybe, that were starting to heal, but she also appeared to have makeup on, so I couldn't tell for sure.

"I'm Wade. You must be Ellie," I said, extending my hand.

She took it, and the soft brush of her skin against my arm sent a jolt through me—not good, because it felt way too nice. Shake it off, soldier.

"Yes, hi. Thanks for helping me out," Ellie said in a cheery voice, though she looked a bit nervous. "I know you're only considering me for the job because of Jack, but I promise you won't regret it. I have plenty of experience with bartending and waitressing."

"Jack already told me you had plenty of experience, so

I'm not worried. Let's get all this paperwork signed, and then I'll show you around the place," I said, knowing full well that Tammy had offered, but I felt the sudden need to do it myself.

I handed over several sheets of paper for her to fill out and sign. While she did, I pretended to do some stuff on my computer but found myself glancing over at her with her eyes looking down. Those definitely looked like healing bruises now that she was up close. Was she in an accident? Jack hadn't mentioned anything.

She had fair skin and bright blue eyes like her brother, but whereas Jack had brown hair, she had light blonde hair that was wavy and landed just past her shoulders. It looked so soft that, I just wanted to run my hands through it.

Inappropriate.

She is your employee now, not to mention your best friend's little sister.

"How old are you?" I asked. I hadn't looked at her résumé yet, but I had a general idea based on how many years younger she was than Jack.

"I just turned twenty-one," she said, looking up at me, and I was immediately captivated by those beautiful blue eyes.

I nodded back. Way too young for my nearly thirty-year-old self, that was for sure.

And Jack's little sister. Remember that.

I tried to distract myself while she finished the paperwork, but I couldn't stop staring.

We got her all set, and then I took her out to show her around the place.

I should have had Tammy do it, but I had this weird compulsion to be near her. I told myself I was just looking after Jack's sister, even though I knew that wasn't it.

We toured the kitchen and the break room in the back. I introduced her to other staff, and then headed out to the bar area and main dining room.

I took her behind the bar to show her where everything was, and for the first time I realized just how tight that space was. Our bar was long and could easily fit two dozen patrons, but the space behind the bar was narrow for the bartenders and staff. With me, Ellie, and Tammy behind there it was cramped. Ellie was right in front of me, and my body vibrated with an odd excitement. She was so close I could smell her perfume. She smelled like lemons and cookies, or maybe that was just her shampoo or something. Whatever it was, my body wanted to be closer.

She and Tammy talked about what was a good time for her to come and shadow the next day while I just stood there awkwardly and stared at her. I could tell she had a great body, even though most of it was hidden behind a bulky T-shirt and jeans. Still, those jeans hugged her curves, emphasizing the attractive figure beneath.

Nope. Don't go there. Jack's sister. Jack's little sister. If I kept repeating it in my mind, hopefully, it would sink in.

"Wade, you good?" I looked up to see Tammy staring at me with a knowing eye.

Yep, she'd caught me looking at Ellie's ass. She just grinned her sneaky little grin at me, and I rolled my eyes.

"Yeah, you good?"

"Yep. She's all yours," Tammy said winking at me. "I'll see you tomorrow, girl," she added, looking at Ellie.

I took Ellie back to the office and grabbed a few things. "We don't have a uniform per se, but everyone just wears these T-shirts with our logo on them. Almost everybody wears them with jeans."

"That's fine," she said, taking the T-shirts I handed over. "We had to be dressed up at my last restaurant, so I'm looking forward to being more comfortable."

Her mouth made a half smile, half smirk. My first thought was to kiss that smirk right off her face.

Damn. Where did that thought come from.

Shut it down.

"Do you have time to show me to Jack's apartment? If not, I can just get the key and show myself in," she said.

That's right. I'd briefly forgotten she was staying in Jack's place until she could find her own.

Great. Just great.

Because Jack's apartment was right next to mine.

"Uh, yeah, I can take you up," I said, grabbing the key from my drawer.

I walked her out the front door of The Watering Hole and to the left side of the building, where the separate entrance for both Ranger Shield Security and the apartments was located. Just inside, a small entryway led to a compact office space on the left and a main hallway that extended toward an elevator.

To the left, a glass door bore the Ranger Shield Security logo, with its name imprinted on the wall beside it. Inside, the front lobby doubled as our reception area—a modest space with a receptionist's desk and a few chairs for waiting clients. Behind the desk were two small conference rooms where we met with clients in person.

Since the glass door was open, I poked my head inside to introduce Ellie to our administrative assistant.

"Ellie, this is Ruthie," I said, motioning toward the woman behind the desk. "She's our receptionist extraordinaire for Ranger Shield Security."

"Hi, it's nice to meet you," Ellie said, stepping forward and offering her hand to Ruthie.

Ruthie replied quietly and calmly, like always. There was definitely a back story to that woman. One of Archer's sticking points about starting this business with us was Ruthie. He'd told us, *She needs a job where she can be safe, so she's our new receptionist*. Vince, Jack, and I knew there was more to the story but dropped it, knowing Archer would tell us when he was ready.

"I didn't know you guys had the security firm up and running already," she said as she turned to me. "Jack talked about you guys starting one, but I didn't know it was already open."

"Since Jack isn't finished with his last tour yet, we've been getting everything up and running, and then he can just jump right in when he gets back," I told her.

We waved goodbye to Ruthie, and walked back out to the entryway.

I pointed to the elevator and gave her a keyring with two keys, as I explained one was for the front entrance door, and the other was for the actual apartment.

As we waited for the elevator, I detailed the rest of the building's layout.

"The elevator goes to the second floor, which is where we have our individual offices, our main security room, and all our tech spaces," I told her as the elevator doors opened.

"You need a key card to access that floor as well as the third floor, which is where the apartments are," I explained while handing her an elevator access key card. "The floor has two separate one-bedroom apartments. One for me and one for Jack, which is now temporarily yours."

Once we got to the third floor, the elevator opened to a small hallway.

"My apartment is on the left, Jack's is on the right," I explained. I opened the door to what would be her apartment until Jack got home and let her in.

"Oh wow," she said, looking around. "I half expected it to be gross and dirty since he's hardly here."

"Nah," I chuckled. "You can take the man out of the military, but you can't take the military out of the man. It's ingrained in us to keep our spaces tidy. Though, saying that, I wouldn't eat anything he left in the fridge unless you're interested in eating a science experiment."

She threw her head back and laughed, and I swore I felt my dick twitch. God, she had a beautiful laugh.

"Once I carry my bags up from the car, I'll clean out the fridge and get some new stuff from the grocery store," she said, giving me a chance to clear my thoughts and focus.

"I can help you with your bags."

"It's not necessary. I didn't bring much," she said.

"I've got it. Let's go," I grunted, perhaps a bit too bluntly, but I needed to get out of this space and maybe get some fresh air.

We walked back down to her car and started unloading her things. Considering she was moving here, she didn't have much—maybe she had more in storage and would bring it when she got her own place.

It only took two trips. As I stepped inside with the last of her bags, I glanced toward the kitchen and spotted her bent over, peering into the fridge. *Damn, she had a great ass.*

Look away.

I quickly turned into the living room just as she straightened up.

"Lucky for me, the fridge contains a few beers and a questionable tub of butter," she said.

I looked up and caught the small smile on her face. God, she was gorgeous. But when she smiled? She was stunning.

This woman was alluring—and she'd absolutely be the star of my fantasies if she weren't my friend's little sister.

Off-limits. You need to bail.

"Okay, well, I gotta get back to the bar. Text me if you need anything," I said as I practically ran out of the door. I needed to separate myself quickly before I did something stupid that I would regret.

Or, more importantly, that Jack would kill me for.

2

ELLIE

I woke early this morning in my new place – at least in my temporary new place. Wondering whether Jack brought women back here and if he had even washed his sheets since, I'd decided to sleep on his couch the first night.

I'd called Katie last night to check in with her and let her know I'd made it safely. She was happy for me that I got away, but I was sad to be far from her. She had been my only close friend since I moved in with my grandma years ago, and I knew I would miss her. I'd told her about meeting Wade, Ruthie, and Tammy and described Jack's boring apartment. Before we hung up, we promised to chat often, even if just via text.

Jack's place was nice and clean. It was a simple one-bedroom apartment, exactly the size I would like to get for myself once my brother was home, albeit with a little more color and character than Jack currently had in his. He wasn't home much, so that explained the bare minimum furniture, but he didn't have any photos or art on the wall, and I was a photo fanatic. His walls were all stark white, and while I usually preferred white walls for good lighting in a bathroom, I would much rather have color on the walls in the other rooms. Gray sheets with a gray comforter. No throw pillows or blankets on the couch. The living room only had a gray couch, a brown coffee table, and a giant TV on top of a black console table. The thing that screamed bachelor pad the most, though, was that he only had wrapped plastic utensils and paper plates in his kitchen.

I needed to run to the store and stock up on a few necessities for the apartment before I met Tammy at the pub for my first shift. I quickly showered and dressed before grabbing my keys and headed out the door.

As I exited the elevator into the lobby space, I saw Ruthie typing away at her desk. Ruthie was a few inches shorter than me. She had silvery blonde hair, much lighter than mine, about an inch or two above her shoulders, and bright, caramel-colored eyes. I waved and said hello, and she smiled back at me.

"Hey Ruthie, is there a place nearby where I can get some basic groceries and maybe a few things for the apartment?" I asked.

"There's a Target and Walmart, both just two miles down the street if that works," she said quietly.

I found myself wondering how she worked as a receptionist when she clearly was uncomfortable talking with people. Maybe I could take some time and chat with her. I didn't know anyone else here, so I could certainly use some new girlfriends. Plus, I would be seeing her almost daily for the next few weeks while I lived here, so it would be polite to get to know her a little better.

"Thanks. Hey Ruthie, would you like to get some lunch together sometime or go shopping?" I asked taking a chance. "I don't know the area, and I would love to know what there is to do around here that's fun."

She stared at me for a few seconds and I realized maybe I had overstepped. She was obviously very shy, so maybe hanging out wasn't really her thing. I was about to tell her never mind when she spoke up, albeit quietly.

"Umm, okay," she said with the faintest smile.

While I gave her my number, I noticed a man standing off to the other side of Ruthie's desk, looking down at his phone. When I listed off my phone number, I noticed the man was now staring right at me. He looked familiar, but I couldn't quite figure out how.

"You must be Ellie," the man said with his hand outstretched. "I'm Archer. I've heard a lot about you from Jack."

Oh! Yes, I remembered Jack talking about him and even showed me a few pictures of him when he was home.

"Hi. It's nice to meet you," I said as I shook his hand.

"If you need anything while you're here, just let Vince, Wade, or me know, okay."

I felt like there was some deeper meaning there, but it was likely him just being nice because I was Jack's sister.

"Thank you. I'll see you guys around," I said as I turned and walked out.

Archer seemed friendly and was definitely attractive. He had the Greek God vibe going. Or maybe Italian or Spanish, I wasn't sure. He had olive-tone skin and black hair that hung a little over his ears and forehead. He was either going for the messy look or was past due to get a haircut.

While Archer was good-looking, he couldn't hold a candle to Wade.

Jack had talked about Archer, Vince, and Wade a lot. Vince and Wade were in his army squadron, and Jack referred to them as his brothers. Archer was Vince's cousin or brother or some kind of relative. He hadn't served overseas with them, but was still part of their tight-knit group. I was happy my brother had them, even if the Army was the reason our relationship was a bit strained.

From what I recalled Jack telling me, Wade was the squad's staff sergeant and a few years older than my brother, but my brother really seemed to admire and respect him. What he hadn't mentioned was how good-looking Wade was. Not that guys thought about stuff like that.

When Tammy first brought me into the office to meet

him, I was amazed at how handsome he was. He had dark brown hair and stunning milk chocolate eyes.

I'm fairly tall myself at 5'9", but he easily had half a foot on me. Even though he was out of the military, he clearly did not miss a workout. He had broad shoulders and muscles upon muscles that looked like they were straining under his black T-shirt. I could see some tattoos peeking out from his sleeves and found myself wanting to rip his shirt off so I could see how far the tattoos went.

I shouldn't be thinking thoughts like that, though. He was Jack's friend, now my boss, and honestly, my track record with men wasn't the greatest lately. As I made my way to the store, I reminded myself that I just needed to focus on myself right now and apply to schools locally. Not think of how smoking hot my new boss was.

Definitely not.

Maybe if I told myself enough, it would actually sink in.

Maybe.

———

After grabbing some new sheets, an extra pillow (Jack only had one), a throw blanket for the bed and one for the couch, some non-plastic silverware, cups, plates, and some groceries to fill the fridge with *real* food, I was set. At least for now.

My hope was that over the next few weeks, I could put some pictures of Jack, Gran, and me in some frames around his place, a houseplant or two, and make this area feel a little homier for him. Not girly, but just more like a home rather than an empty place to just eat and sleep.

I pulled my hair into a ponytail and tried to do my best to cover up what remained of my bruises and marks on my neck before heading down to the pub to meet Tammy. As soon as I walked in the door, her loud but friendly voice greeted me.

"Heya, Ellie. Come on over, dear," Tammy yelled and waved me over to the bar.

Tammy seemed like a super sweet lady from what I could tell. She was short, especially compared to me, with a stocky, muscular build. Her dark brown hair was accented by a few strands of gray, and the slight wrinkles around her eyes suggested she might be in her mid-forties. Yet, everything else about her gave the impression she was ten years younger.

"Let's get you ready so you can start earning us some big tips. We share them, by the way," she told me, leaning in. "I have a feeling you are gonna be making our tip jar nice and full."

"Thanks, Tammy." I laughed at her confidence, but I appreciated her faith in me. "I'll do what I can to pull my weight around here and help out as much as you need me."

"Glad to hear it!" Tammy said excitedly. "Wade told me you can work pretty much any time, any day. Is that correct? Because I make the schedule mostly, and then Wade just approves it."

"Yeah, I'm trying to save up to go to college, so I'll take any and all shifts you can give me, both at the bar and waiting tables. I'm not picky," I said shaking my head.

She showed me around, and then after getting a refill for the only customer currently at the bar, she wiped down the counters and informed me the lunch rush would start soon.

"Are you transferring from another school or just getting started?" she asked, with no judgment in her voice, but I still felt a little embarrassed at how my situation had delayed me going to school.

"Umm...life got in the way a little bit the last year, so I had to put school on the back burner for a bit, but hopefully I can find someplace not too far from here and apply there," I told her.

Her eyes softened, and she leaned over and put her hand on my hand, where I was restocking glasses.

"Does this delayed start have anything to do with those bruises I see healing on you?" she whispered to me.

My eyes widened as I stared at her. Crap. I guess I hadn't done as good of a job as I thought on covering them with my makeup. I didn't know what to say.

"It's okay, sweetheart. You can tell me when you're good and ready," she said calmly. "But if you need me to take care of him, I listen to a lot of true crime podcasts, so I know exactly how to kill a man and bury the body where no one will find it," she said, winking at me and then turning toward the bar back area.

I half-chuckled, not really knowing whether Tammy meant that or not.

I wasn't sure I wanted to find out.

I tried to change the subject, so I asked her to tell me about herself.

"Not much about me, girl," she started, shrugging, and I could tell she didn't like sharing about herself. "I was an Army brat growing up, and then kept it in the family and went into the Army myself. I used to come here to this pub a lot in between deployments. Got to know Wade's uncle, and when I retired, he offered me a job. Got good retirement from the military, but I'm not the type of person to just sit around and be lazy all day. Plus, I like talking to people, and a bar is a great place for that."

I could believe that. She definitely seemed like a talker – and a friendly one at that – though I wondered if she had a boyfriend or kids or anything.

"Well, enough about my boring life. What are you going to school for? Have you decided?" she asked.

I saw what she was doing here. Flipping the conversation so she didn't have to talk about herself, so I let it go. I understood what that was like, not wanting to talk about certain aspects of my life, either.

"Massage therapy school," I started to explain. "I found a few schools that offer a program starting soon, and even with me only taking classes part-time, I could still graduate in less than two years."

"Girl, you ever need a volunteer test dummy, I'm your girl," Tammy said as she stopped what she was doing with a glass in hand and turned to me. "Everything on my body aches these days. Hell, just thinking about all my aches and pains makes my head hurt. I'll be a great client."

I laughed as she nodded at me and turned to go grab a menu for a guy who'd just sat down.

"I'll give you a massage, Tammy, any time you want," the new customer grinned like a Cheshire cat.

This man sat down at the very end of the bar, and appeared to be at least fifteen years older than Tammy, but friendly.

"As tempting of an offer as that is, Eddie, I know where your hands have been and I don't want them anywhere near my body," she said, winking at him and grinning as though this was a joke between them.

He guffawed loudly and clearly didn't take her rejection to heart.

"I'm just happy it's you two pretty ladies workin' behind the bar tonight instead of the usual scruffy ones," Eddie said. "I'll take my usual, Tammy-girl."

Tammy laughed and must have seen the confusion on my face.

"He's talking about Corey and Sam, our other two main bartenders," Tammy explained. "Sam works here and goes to school part-time. Speakin' of which, you may want to ask him about schools if you're interested."

"Oh, thanks, I may just do that," I told her.

She continued while filling a beer for Eddie. "Corey works here and also at the gym down the street as a personal trainer. I teach a few martial arts classes there, which is how he found this job. Now, let's get to it. You can start by getting that new customer down there, and then I'll show you the rest as we go through the day."

If the rest of the shift was similar to how it began, this was going to be a great job. I liked Tammy already and was looking forward to meeting everyone else. And maybe, just maybe, working a little more with Wade.

3

ELLIE

I'd only been working at the pub for a little more than a week, but I had already started to recognize the regulars from everyone else. The pub was packed, and while my current shift had only started about two hours ago, it already felt like it had been closer to eight. But this place was great. It had some Irish pub vibes, with a rustic, cozy atmosphere to it.

Due to the proximity to the Dobbington Air Reserve Base down the street, there was a strong military theme. Vintage military uniforms and equipment like helmets and canteens decorated the walls. Just above the bar, a World War II parachute canopy hung from the ceiling. It definitely gave it a unique setting.

The Irish pub vibes came more from the old, worn hardwood floors, the warm but dim lighting, and exposed wood beams and posts. All the tables and the bar top were made of dark wood and many of them had names of soldiers who had been killed or lost overseas carved into them. The various military logos or slogans were also carved into some of the tables, some even scratched out and written over in a bit of a friendly rivalry sort of thing.

I hadn't seen Wade since that first day. Tammy said he spent most of his time holed up in the back office or up on the second floor, helping Archer and Vince with security stuff. I couldn't help but feel he might also be avoiding me.

One person who was not avoiding me was Ruthie. She and I chatted almost every day as I went to and from the building. She always asked about the pub. How my shifts were going. What it was like working for Wade. That last question was hard since we didn't work much together, but he was always friendly. Ruthie and I had planned to actually go out after work today on the Chattahoochee River for a hike, and I was looking forward to it.

I rotated between shifts behind the bar or out on the floor waiting tables I liked working behind the bar more because I got to work with Tammy, and she was a hoot. She bantered just as easily with new customers as she did with regulars. She was the perfect combination of friendly and sassy. She had an easy charm to her, but also had no problem cutting people off who'd had too much to drink or started getting too rowdy.

I'd met all the other employees by now, too. Chuck, the main cook in the evenings, was a big, burly dude, who apparently had worked here almost as long as Tammy. He was a great chef, but not great with people, so staying in the kitchen, I'd learned, was perfect for him.

I'd only met Sam briefly, but fully planned to pick his brain as much as possible about the colleges here so I could get back to that goal as soon as possible.

Several of the wait staff were also students around my age and all seemed very friendly, including Beth, whom I'd been chatty with during the last few shifts. There were also two other waitresses who had been here for more than a decade.

Tammy and I had just finished the lunch rush and were trying to clean things up a bit and get ahead before the happy hour crowd came in.

The phone rang, and I grabbed it since I was closer.

"Hello, this is the Watering Hole. How can I help you?" I said, but there was just silence.

I swore I could hear someone breathing, but there were no words.

"Hello? Is anybody there?" I asked again. Still nothing, so I hung it up, figuring someone probably had the wrong number and went back to cleaning.

"Please tell me that wasn't somebody else calling in sick," Tammy inquired.

"No, I think it was a butt dial," I told her. "Who called in sick?"

"Sam is out tonight, so the boss-man is comin' in to do bar duty for the late shift," she said as she took out clean glasses and filled the shelves with them.

I found myself a little nervous, knowing that Wade

was coming in. Since I'd worked the mid-day shift, I would only work with him for about two hours, but there was just something about Wade that brought a sensation to my body that I had never felt before. Sure, he was attractive, but it felt like more than that. Likely it was just his connection to Jack, or at least that's what I was telling myself.

"Since I'm about to clock out, why don't you take the group that just sat down at the end of the bar, and I'll finish out Hank's tab," Tammy said.

Hank was one of our regulars. In his late sixties, he flirted endlessly with every female employee who served him, but he was super sweet and tipped very well.

I nodded to Tammy and walked over to the far end of the bar to what appeared to be three guys in their military fatigues. We tended to get a lot of military men and women here. In fact, the base usually brought us about half our clientele.

"Hey guys, what can I get you?" I asked as I slid some coasters in front of them.

"How about a Coke and your phone number, gorgeous," the first one said with a wink.

Internally, I groaned, but this was part of the job.

"Gentlemen, I saw her first," Hank piped in, looking straight at the man who just asked for my number. "I've been asking her for two weeks and knowin' how sexy I am–" he paused and rubbed his beer belly, "–if she won't give her number to *me*, she probably won't give it to you," he said with a wink back at me.

All three of them chuckled, and I winked back at Hank, knowing he was doing it just so I wouldn't have to turn the man down awkwardly.

"Sorry. Apparently, my number belongs to Hank," I said, smiling at the three guys in front of me.

I got their drink and appetizer orders and then turned around and typed the order into the computer.

"Those guys giving you a hard time?" a low voice rumbled in my ear.

I whirled around and came face-to-face with Wade. He was so close and smelled so good. I just stared at him dumbly. Then I realized he was waiting for me to say something, but I couldn't remember what he asked.

"Uh...what?" I asked.

He turned his head and stared in the direction of the guys at the bar. "The guys at the end of the bar. Are they bothering you?"

"Oh, uh, n-no," I stuttered.

Get it together, girl.

"They, uh, asked for my number, but Hank put them in their place," I said with a small smile. "Even if he hadn't, I've worked in bars long enough. I know how to take care of myself."

He nodded, but then turned back to the men, and his eyes narrowed a bit. He stayed close to me, and I found myself needing to break the tension currently rolling through his body.

"Though I didn't realize the Air Force had similar uniforms to the Army," I told Wade.

"What do you mean?" He looked back at me with furrowed brows.

"Their uniforms," I said, nodding over in their direction. "They look a lot like Jack's, but I thought Dobbington was an Air Force base," I explained.

He nodded in understanding.

"Dobbington is the 22nd Air Force headquarters, but it's also home to Navy operations support, Army Reserve, Marine Reserve, and Georgia National Guard," he said.

"Oh wow, I had no idea." I looked up at him and smiled. "Thanks for the lesson."

Wade and I stayed busy at the bar and didn't chat much for the next two hours, but I found myself drawn to him. Each time I caught his gaze, he was always looking right at me. When I glanced over at him, I could have sworn I caught him looking at my ass.

When he leaned over the bar, chatting with a customer, his arms stretched out as he grabbed the edge of the bar, I took a moment to fully soak him in.

God, when his arms flexed like that, I swore something in me just tingled. I continued to stare at him for a few more beats while pretending to rinse the same glass I had been rinsing for several minutes now, but I just couldn't turn away. Even his butt looked great in those jeans. He looked like sex on a stick, as Katie would say. He straightened and turned toward me. I looked away before we could make eye contact, knowing if we did my face would be multiple shades of red.

I was wiping down the counter and about to take

some empty plates to the back when Wade came up next to me. God, he smelled so good. His scent of musk, bourbon, and the great outdoors were intoxicating. When he neared my body buzzed with need and excitement.

"Go ahead and closeout, and I'll take it from here," he rumbled, startling me out of my deep and inappropriate thoughts.

"Oh...umm...are you sure?" I asked and looked around at several people still at the bar. "We're still pretty busy I don't mind staying for a bit." As flustered as I was being around him, I found myself wanting to stay and keep working next to him just a little longer.

"No, I'm good. Go ahead," he said, though his face seemed strained as though he wasn't sure if he wanted me to go or not. But I wasn't going to force my company on him just because I had this irrational urge to stay.

"Okay. I'm going hiking with Ruthie so thanks," I told him.

I closed myself out from the register and finished cleaning up my portion of the bar. Then I went to the back to grab my purse and phone and saw Beth sitting in the breakroom.

"Hey, Ellie," she said smiling. "Boss-man treating you okay? He's chattier with you than he is with the rest of us, but that's not always a good thing with a boss."

"Really?" I asked, because I would not classify Wade as chatty, and I told her that. "It might be because of my brother."

She looked at me with a confused face. I chuckled and

told her that Wade had served with my brother, which was how I found the job. I added that I was staying at his place upstairs until he came back from overseas.

"Ahhh, okay. That makes more sense." She nodded and continued to drink her water. "He hardly ever says much unless it's to Tammy, but she's got a way of making anyone talk, and he and Sam just usually grunt at each other like some weird bro code."

I laughed because it was so true.

"But he's cute, don't you think?" she asked.

I wasn't sure how to answer that. I definitely found him attractive, but he was the boss. Were we supposed to say that about the boss? Plus, I didn't need to be thinking about a man like that. The last time I did that, it was a disaster. I decided to just ignore my lustful thoughts toward my boss and focus on me.

"I guess, if you like that sort of look," I said to Beth while shrugging, hoping my indifference would play down the reality of my thoughts.

She looked at me like she thought I was crazy. Not wanting to give her more time to ask questions, I grabbed my bag, said goodbye, and then made my way out. I didn't look at the bar as I passed it but instead pulled out my phone to text Katie and see how she was doing. I knew she was getting ready to go on vacation with her family soon and she needed the break.

I felt eyes on me as I reached the door. I turned around and saw Wade's eyes locked with mine. I smiled and waved at him like a total dork and then walked out.

He grinned back at me, and let me tell you...Wade was gorgeous when he wasn't smiling, but when he grinned like that with a hint of wickedness, he was downright dangerous to a woman's self-control. I definitely needed to be careful around him, especially since my focus right now needed to be on myself, not a man.

Just under an hour later, Ruthie and I were walking through the entrance to the main trail at the river park. I was stunned at how beautiful it was and how many trees there were. It was summer, and a very hot one, but with all the trees providing shade it felt at least fifteen degrees cooler on this trail, which made it very pleasant.

"Atlanta is called a city in a forest," Ruthie informed me.

"I admit I haven't ventured out much, but if the rest of the city looks like this, I would believe that," I confirmed.

"Supposedly fifty percent of Atlanta is covered in trees, which makes it one of the most forested cities or something like that," Ruthie informed me. "Wade and Vince are both from here originally, so when I first moved here, they filled me with all kinds of facts about the city."

"I'm surprised you could get that much out of Wade. He's not very chatty, at least not to me," I noted, and also, admittedly said it to fish for information. She also worked with him, but in a different capacity, so she may have some insight.

She laughed a little. "So true. Honestly, none of them are particularly chatty, unless they're complaining to me about paperwork. Then, suddenly they're all chatty and telling me how awesome I am and how I would be their favorite person in the *whole world* if I did their paperwork for them. Especially Wade. Based off the paperwork I do for him, we should be besties by now."

I knew she meant it in a joking manner, but I couldn't help but feel a bit of jealousy about that. I shouldn't, but there was definitely a twinge of envy in me. Part of me wanted to offer to help with the paperwork to ease his burden. He'd done so much for me already. It would be nice to help him out. At least that was the reason I told myself I would be doing it.

Ruthie and I walked for another forty minutes or so, chatting and taking in the sights. I didn't realize how much I'd needed this. It felt good to get out in the fresh air. It felt good to make a new friend. I also found myself wondering what it would be like to hike with Wade out here and just sit on one of the benches along the river. Maybe one day I would work up the courage to ask him. On second thought, maybe that wasn't the smartest idea since he was my boss.

4

WADE

I stared at the endless abyss of paperwork that was sitting on my desk, willing me to finish it, and realized I would rather do anything else. My mind drifted to last night—it had been my first time working with Ellie.

I had been intentionally trying to avoid shifts with her because every time she was near all I seemed to do was picture her naked and other inappropriate things. So, in an effort to avoid temptation, I arranged the schedule so she and I wouldn't work the same shift. Instead, I spent most of my time holed up in the back office or upstairs with Archer and Vince when Ellie was on shift.

Yesterday, however, when Sam called in sick, I had no choice but to step in and work with her.

If I was being honest, yes, when I asked her to leave last night, we were still pretty busy, but I needed Ellie to go. She was a great employee, but I was getting twitchy being in such a close space with her. My body craved being next to her, and every time a strand of her hair fell loose from behind her ear, I had to keep myself from reaching over and pushing it back in place.

I recalled the moment about an hour into my shift when I had been leaning over the bar talking to Diego Martin, one of our regulars, when he grinned and told me the new girl was checking out my ass. There was only one person he could mean – Ellie. I decided at that moment to have her clock out and head home. Any longer of her standing next to me, especially knowing she was checking me out, could lead to me doing something stupid.

Then she smiled and waved goodbye to me as she walked out the door, and I was a goner. I grinned like a high school boy. My dick twitched, and I realized maybe I needed to get laid. Otherwise, that woman was going to be the death of me.

"You don't strike me as the type to shit where you eat," Diego had said to me as I'd watched Ellie leave. He must have taken my pause to mean I didn't understand, so he'd explained further. *"I mean, you don't seem like the kind to sleep with someone you work with."*

"I knew what you meant," I'd told him. *"And no, I don't. Plus, she's Jack's little sister."*

"Ahh. The other guy in the security company?" he'd asked. *"The one who's still overseas?"*

I'd nodded.

"Well, uh, I was asking 'cause if you weren't gonna ask her out, I was going to, but maybe not just in case I do decide to work with you," he's said, a huge grin on his face.

I'd known it was just a casual remark, but the thought of him asking her out had made me irrationally pissed off.

I had no claim to her, and Diego seemed like a nice guy, so it wasn't even like I could claim I was protecting her from some asshole. I tried not to think too hard about why that had bothered me all night.

My thoughts of last night were interrupted by someone opening my office door. As the handle turned and the door opened, I stood up from my chair, ready to give Tammy or Beth hell since neither of them ever knocked before coming in, when I saw Ellie walk in and slide to the small couch to the right of the door in front of my desk. She must have seen my movement, though, because she let out a small shriek and instantly fell to the ground, purse thrown down with her hands covering her head like she was expecting me to attack her.

"Ellie, it's just me," I said, finding her reaction a bit odd.

Her eyes opened and she looked up at me as red color began to fill in the paleness of her face.

"Oh God, Wade, I'm so sorry," she said, slowly rising from her spot on the ground.

I walked around and held out my hand to help her up. She grabbed onto it, and I felt a warm current move through my hand and arm. It felt nice, and I didn't want to let her hand go, but I needed to or this would become awkward.

"I didn't know you were in here or I would have

knocked." She took the hand that I had just touched and put it to her chest.

She closed her eyes and took a few deep breaths like she was attempting to calm herself down.

Feeling guilty for scaring her, even though it wasn't my fault she didn't knock. I softened my voice a bit to ask her why she was here.

"Did you need something?" I asked and noticed her hands were shaking slightly.

"Sorry, I was just going to leave a small note on your desk," she said and held up a small piece of paper. "Though I might as well just tell you in person now."

She handed me the paper and spoke again. "My brother called this morning and told me to tell you thanks for helping me get moved and settled in here. I know he feels guilty he's overseas and couldn't help, so he wanted me to tell you how much it means to him that you helped me. He cherishes your friendship."

"Did he really say cherished?" I asked, because I doubted her brother would have used that sappy word.

"Well, I'm paraphrasing," she said and shook her hands in front of her face as though that explained everything.

She seemed oddly nervous and tucked that loose piece of hair behind her ear again. My fingers twitched to do it for her. It would be easy to do since I was only a foot in front of her. I hadn't moved back after helping her up off the floor. Being this close, I could smell whatever her perfume was and she smelled like a cupcake. Or maybe that was just her natural scent. Vanilla and lemons. I needed to back up and get back to paperwork, though I didn't want to do either. What I really wanted to do was touch that loose piece of hair that had popped out again, then slide my hand to the back of her neck and kiss that glossy stuff off her lips.

Shut that thought down.

"How was your hike with Ruthie yesterday?" I asked, hoping to change the topic and clear my brain of inappropriate thoughts of her.

She looked at me, and a smile took over her face once my question registered to her.

"It was great," she noted. "That trail by the river is beautiful. So many trees and plants, and the walkways were nice and wide, so you didn't get run over by people on bikes. There were also dozens of people on kayaks and floats on the river."

"Yeah, I've done that a few times. It's fun," thinking back to summers in high school.

My friends and I would go down to the river with our small floats and innertubes, get some beer we stole from one of our parents' stashes, and just meander downstream for a few hours.

"It looked like it," she said wistfully. "You should come next time."

As soon as the words left her mouth, she pinched her lips closed and suddenly looked nervous—

like she hadn't meant to say that out loud.

"I mean, Ruthie said Archer comes sometimes, so

um...maybe you could come too," she stuttered. "Like, um, since you're friends, you could maybe hang out there. With us. For a hike or whatever."

She sighed, tilting her head down. "Sorry, I blabber when I'm nervous."

"Why are you nervous?" I asked, thinking to myself how cute she was all flustered like this.

Her head popped up, and she looked at me, but didn't say anything. That curl popped out from behind her ear again, and I couldn't resist. I leaned forward and tucked it behind her ear for her. I heard her take a deep breath, and her eyes darkened a little. Her eyes dropped to my mouth and I could practically hear her brain thinking. Her eyes moved back to mine and she licked her lips.

God, this woman was going to be the death of me. My office here at the pub was already tiny to begin with, but with Ellie in here, it felt even smaller. The windowless walls felt like they were shrinking around us, forcing her into my space. Feeling her pull, I took a half step forward into her space.

"Wade," she whispered. I wasn't sure if it was a warning, or an invitation, the way she said it.

She licked her lips again, and I knew I had to kiss her. I leaned in as I reached back out to slide a hand behind her neck.

"Boss man, you got a delivery!" Tammy's voice yelled from outside my office.

Ellie gasped and stepped back.

"Umm...I'm going to go back out and umm, help

Tammy, for our uh shift. Yeah." Ellie stammered and grabbed her bag off the floor before leaving my office.

When she opened the door, Tammy was standing there with a big grin on her face. She just stood there staring at me for a few moments.

"I didn't interrupt anything important, did I?" she asked, but that sly grin on her face told me she knew Ellie was in here and her yelling was her version of a heads up.

"What do you need?" I questioned her, my voice a little gruff.

"Just wanted to let you know the alcohol delivery came and I signed for it. It's all in the stock room, but I know you said you wanted to know as soon as it got here. Going back to the bar now. Let me know if you need anything else," She turned and walked back to the front of the restaurant, smirking the whole way.

My office was now quiet with only myself inside. *What the hell just happened?* I'm mad at myself for getting caught almost kissing an employee. What bothered me more was how disappointed I felt at not having the opportunity to kiss her.

Needing to change focus, I moved my line of sight back to the payroll paperwork in front of me. The idea of assembling IKEA furniture without instructions seemed more appealing than this. I needed to hire someone to deal with this paperwork. Bills and invoices were not my thing. Plus, it was getting harder and harder to do administrative paperwork for the pub and also work for the security business.

Ranger Shield Security was taking off, with clients starting to pour in. Most of them were cases of a husband or wife looking to dig up dirt on their spouse ahead of an impending divorce, or picking up some high dollar skips, which we passed off to Vince since his dad was a bounty hunter and had taught his son everything he needed to know.

The uptick in clients was good, but with Jack still deployed, we needed to think about hiring an extra hand or two. The guy at the bar the day before, Diego, was someone I'd had had my eye on. He'd finished active duty and was currently on reserve. He was a tech whiz, and from what I'd learned, his role in the military had been gathering intel, so he would be a great addition to the company since tech ops weren't really Vince's strong suit or mine. Jack had some skills in that, but with him being away, that didn't help us much in the short term.

I also needed to reach out to my sister, Willa. She worked as a forensic accountant, but that meant she worked with a lot of skilled tech people, and she'd mentioned interviewing someone for an open tech position at their office. If she didn't hire the person, maybe we could.

Willa and her husband Paul lived here in Georgia, too, though I didn't see them as much as I should. She was older than me by two years and had married Paul right out of college. They had two kids—Charlie and Haley.

I wanted what she had, a family, but I knew that would never happen for me. Not because of my job but because of the monster I could be, sometimes without warning. Which made me think back to Candace.

During my first tour, I met Candace while I was home on break. We hit it off and decided to keep in touch each time I came home between deployments. It wasn't anything serious, but we enjoyed each other's company. Especially naked company.

When I would come home on leave between deployments, we would grab a bite to eat and head back to either one of our apartments, but we never stayed the night. She said she liked sleeping in her own bed, and I didn't like the seriousness it conveyed to women when I stayed the night.

I didn't want a relationship while I was overseas in case something happened to me. I saw it happen to many other guys. But one night, it was storming really bad, so I let her crash at my place.

That night, I had a nightmare and apparently elbowed her hard in the side while sleeping. I felt terrible, and even slept on the couch the rest of the night. The nightmares had been coming increasingly frequently since my last mission overseas. I lost men during a special ops assignment went bad in Jalalabad, Afghanistan. The explosion killed two of my men, and injured two more.

I knew this was likely PTSD but hadn't wanted to see a therapist because then people talked, and I didn't want to leave my men stranded because the brass had pulled me off a mission for being weak.

I didn't want to risk hurting her again, so I stuck with my rule of not sleeping together.

A few months later, she happened to be at the same bar I was at with friends. She only lived three blocks away, so we walked back to her place. I blame the alcohol, because after a few rounds of sex, we both must have fallen asleep, and I woke up to her scream after I had another nightmare and punched her in the shoulder and neck. I left her place feeling horrible and was walking back to the bar to get my car when a text from her came through, saying to please lose her number.

I didn't blame her. I couldn't control what I did during my dreams. Even though it had been unintentional, I couldn't bear the thought of hurting a woman.

So, while I wasn't swearing off women entirely, I just didn't have sleepovers, and that ultimately meant no relationships since, after a while, women tended to want that. And I was too messed up for that.

The nightmares have become less frequent now that I started seeing a therapist, but they weren't zero. Until then, I wasn't going to take a chance with staying the night with a woman. And while the therapy as helping, I wasn't sure I would ever get to the point of zero nightmares. That was why Ellie and I would never happen. I had to shut that thought down.

It also didn't help that if Jack knew that I was thinking of his sister naked, he would likely cut off my balls. Or worse. Ellie was also the type of woman who deserved a relationship, and I couldn't give that to her.

So, I put all inappropriate thoughts of her away, no matter how hard that was. With that said, it didn't mean I had to help other guys have a chance. So, for now, I wasn't going to give Diego or any other guy at the pub any help with Ellie either.

Selfish? Definitely.

Did I care? Not one bit.

5

ELLIE

It was loud. Louder than usual, even for a Friday night. Way busier than we were a few nights ago when I worked briefly with Wade. Tammy and I were behind the bar, and even though it was busy, she and I had developed a great flow between us that made the shift go so smoothly.

She was friendly and quick-witted, and I genuinely enjoyed working with her. We generally split the bar down in half, and each picked a side to cover while also filling drink orders from the waiters and waitresses, but on occasion, we would cross over the middle line if one of us got busy or we knew the people on the other side. Really, it was just if Tammy knew them because I still didn't really know anyone here, at least not anyone that would come visit me at the bar.

"You mind if I grab the good-lookin' one with the goatee and tight black shirt in the corner over on your side?" Tammy asked, pointing at a man who looked about her age.

"Sure, no problem," I told her. "You know him?"

"Not yet, but hopefully I will by the end of the night."

I laughed and told her to watch out for that one because his muscles looked like they could break through his tight shirt at any moment.

"I like my men like I like my coffee – strong enough to pick me up. And he will definitely be able to do that," Tammy said with a sly grin on her face. "Though, saying that, I also don't want them lookin' like something I drew with my left hand, which is usually what happens when I pick 'em online."

I couldn't help but chuckle at her descriptions and headed over to grab some more freshly washed glasses to dry them.

Ruthie had come over after work and was sitting at the bar on my side. I appreciated the fact that she came, because I knew she worked long hours over at Ranger Shield's front desk. Every time I would pass by the front office, whether on my way to or from the apartment she seemed to be there.

"I keep meaning to tell you every time I see you that I like your necklace," I told her as I pointed to the two little pale pink boxing gloves hanging from a silver chain around her neck.

She grabbed the charm between her fingers as she looked down at it.

"Archer gave it to me when we came here," she said

and then paused. "It's to remind me that I'm a fighter." Her words were strong, yet there was definitely emotion in her voice.

"I'm not much of a pink person, but it's really cute, and it suits you," I told her, smiling.

"Thanks." She smiled back at me, small at first, but then she straightened her head and smiled even bigger. "I like your necklace too."

I looked down at my charm necklace and smiled.

"My grandma gave it to me so I could add charms that would tell the story of my life," I told her. "I miss her so much, but it's been nice to have this keepsake to remind me of her."

"That's awesome," Ruthie said to me with a sad smile.

We didn't get to chat too much more since more customers started to trickle in, but any free moment I had, I made my way over to her to get to know her better. I learned she was born and raised in Vegas, and moved here at the same time as Archer since he offered her a job, which she was happy about since her grandpa lived in Georgia, too. Sadly, her mom had died when she was young, just like mine, and she also had an older brother like me. The difference was she did not seem close to her family she had left at all. When I asked about them, her response had been, "Don't know, don't care."

We found we both shared a love of rom-coms and decided that we would see one at the theater soon. We also made plans to go back to the Chattahoochee National Forest in a few days to try out a new trail. My parents had taken Jack and me to Gatlinburg and Great Smokey Mountain National Park when we were kids, and I loved it. I loved the outdoors. I was glad Ruthie did too.

Tammy bumped her hip into mine with a drink in each hand and nodded her head toward the back. "Phone call for you Blondie."

"Who is it?" I asked, but Tammy was already on the other side of the bar handing the drinks over to her customers and chatting them up.

I walked over and picked it up, wondering who on Earth would call me here since the people I was closest to would just call my cell. Granted, I always kept my cell underneath the counter at the back of the bar so I wouldn't be distracted by it while on shift.

"Hello," I said, but there was no response. "Hello. This is the Watering Hole. How can I help you?" I said again, but there was nothing. I hung up and figured it was just kids playing a prank, so I walked back over to Ruthie to refill her drink up.

"Who was on the phone?" Tammy asked as she winked at me. "He sounded like he could be handsome."

"How can you tell that over the phone?" I laughed.

"Honey, I've been on this Earth for four decades. I can definitely tell which ones sound handsome and which ones don't just by their voice," she said, sounding so confident. "Now, my problem is, I tend to let the handsome face overrule all the other red flags that usually go with the smooth voice," she said as she laughed.

I could sympathize. I'd definitely missed all the red flags with Randall.

"Same. I feel ya on that," Ruthie chimed in, and then leaned forward and stage-whispered to Tammy and me, "So, tell us more about your gentleman caller."

I laughed at the enthusiasm coming from both of them and just shook my head.

"Whoever it was must have hung up, because there was no one there by the time I got to the phone."

"That's a shame. We need to get you back out there and have a little fun." Tammy said with a smirk.

"I don't exactly have a great track record, and right now I need to focus on myself and starting school," I told them, though if I was being truthful, it was also because the only man my brain seemed to be interested in anymore was Wade. Given he was my boss, not to mention Jack's good friend, meant he was off-limits.

"Honey, I'm not trying to marry you off," Tammy said, grinning like a loon. "Sometimes one magical night with a good-lookin' man is exactly what the doctor ordered." She winked and pointed at me, then made her way back to the muscled man with the goatee she had been flirting with tonight.

"That's exactly what got me in trouble the last time," I mumbled under my breath, but it must not have been too quiet, because Tammy's smile disappeared.

"Ellie, you listen to me," she said in her mothering tone. "We all make mistakes in life, but we learn from those mistakes and come out better on the other side. You also can't let those mistakes keep you from living."

"Amen, Tammy!" Ruthie chimed in.

I knew she was right, but once you've been burned, it's hard to re-program your brain into trying again.

"Tell ya what." She snapped her fingers, and her face lit up like she had the greatest idea in the world. "When you find a man, you think might fit the bill, we'll have Wade and his boys run a quick background check on him and make sure he doesn't have any outstanding warrants, or a second family in another state or something!"

"Or one of those guys who posts cringey dance videos on TikTok," Ruthie added, her face twisted like she'd just bitten into a sour lemon.

Yeah, I'm never going to ask Wade to run a background check on a guy.

Reason number one, he would tell Jack, and I didn't need my brother knowing all the details of my love life.

Reason number two, background checks didn't tell you everything. I was pretty sure Randall's job at the bank required a background check, and it probably hadn't told them the monster he could be behind closed doors.

Reason number three, my interest in Wade would make that all kinds of awkward.

"Speaking of which, maybe having a fun night with one of the boys upstairs would be good, Lord knows they are all super handsome, and single," Tammy said, fanning her face with her hand as Ruthie laughed behind me. "They're all too young for me, but the minute he brings one in that's closer to my age, I'm gonna take my chance, hop on that horse and ride him into the sunset."

Ruthie and I chuckled at her bold declaration, but Tammy wasn't done.

She sighed dramatically, placing a hand over her chest. "I mean, it's been a while, ladies. At this point, I'd settle for a man who knows how to use power tools and doesn't breathe like a dying walrus when he sleeps."

I snorted. "Tammy, your standards are both oddly specific and concerning."

Tammy shrugged. "Listen, I'm a woman of simple needs. A strong back, decent stamina, and the ability to kill a spider without screaming. That's all I ask."

Ruthie shook her head, laughing. "I'll make sure to tell Wade to start recruiting accordingly."

Tammy pointed a finger at Ruthie. "You do that. And if he finds one with salt-and-pepper hair and forearms that look like they could split firewood? Give him my number immediately."

"What are y'all talking about over here?" Beth said as she came over to the bar to pick up some drinks.

"Men," Tammy said, then turned to me. "This one here said she doesn't want a man right now, but I think that's exactly what she needs."

"I just got out of a relationship," I told Beth. "I just want to focus on myself right now and school."

"You do you, girl, and don't let Tammy persuade you otherwise," Beth said, then walked back to her table.

"You want me to talk to Wade," Tammy started to say, but I jumped in.

"No!" I said, probably a little too quickly. "He's my boss, which would be all kinds of weird. Plus, that would be awkward with him being friends with my brother."

"Honey..." She grinned at me conspiratorially. "I meant I was gonna talk to Wade about any of his single friends, but interesting that your brain went in that direction," Tammy said, smirking, and I knew I had said too much.

"Yes, very interesting," Ruthie chimed in.

Ruthie stared at me, suspicion written all over her face. I decided to get back to my customers and ignore Tammy, Beth, and Ruthie before I said anything else stupid.

I also tried not to think about Wade, but I kept finding my thoughts going back to him. How kind he had been to me, how ruggedly handsome he was, how I seemed drawn to him whenever he was near. Yeah, definitely not thinking about him. Just as I felt I was getting a handle on not thinking about Wade, the universe had other plans.

I was in the middle of pouring a beer when Tammy's voice caught my attention.

"Hey, boss-man, I changed a few things on the schedule. Take a look and tell me what you think," Tammy said as Wade walked by the bar.

"Just here to drop off a few things off, but I'll take a look real quick," he replied, briefly looking at me, giving me a chin lift but saying nothing, then he walked back through the employee door—likely headed to his office.

He wore a charcoal gray polo shirt with dark jeans and looked so good. His beard appeared freshly trimmed, but his hair could've used a cut. He was more dressed up than usual, and I wondered if he had an important meeting for the security business today. Trying to bring my thoughts back to something else, I turned to one of my customers and took their order.

Minutes later, I heard Wade's voice behind me and Tammy talking back to him, but I was trying to write down the order and not screw it up, so I didn't turn around until after their exchange was clearly done. When I finally looked over, Wade was on his way out, but stopped to chat with a booth full of women. They were all dolled up, and one was now standing next to Wade, her hand stroked his arm in a very familiar way.

I found myself getting irrationally angry at the thought of that woman touching him. I tried to focus on putting the order into the computer and not staring at them, but my eyes kept flitting over from time to time. Wade didn't seem to be encouraging her touching, but he also wasn't stopping her either. He seemed to know her or was at least familiar with her based on his body language. An old girlfriend, maybe? Occasional booty-call?

"No matter how hard you hit those buttons, it won't make the food come out faster," Tammy said beside me.

I looked up at her to find her looking at me, then glancing over at Wade, then back at me.

"For what it's worth, that girl is a regular customer," she said quietly. "She flirts with him all the time, but as far as I know, he hasn't done anything with it."

She patted me on the shoulder and walked back to grab some empty glasses and dishes from her side of the bar before I could sputter out any kind of comment— whether to defend my thoughts or pretend I wasn't angry. As I watched Wade talk to that woman, I sighed and tried to clear the jealousy from my mind. I needed to get my focus on myself right now, not a man. I told myself I wasn't going to look back over at them.

"God, what a hussy," Beth hissed as she walked up to my side of the counter to pick up her drink order.

I glanced up at her to see she was also looking at Wade.

"That woman comes in here all the time, making a scene with Wade," Beth continued unprompted. "All up on him, being a bitch to the rest of us servers if she can't have Wade personally bring her drinks out. Then, when she gets stuck sitting in one of our sections, she's a horrible tipper and crazy rude. Such a pain in my ass. The only good part is watching her face every time he turns her down."

She left no room for comment, grabbing her drinks and walking away. Her parting words put a small smile on my face—especially when I looked up to see Wade step-ping out the door. The woman frowned as she sank back into her seat.

I wasn't proud of my initial reaction to the so-called "hussy," but I'd be lying if I said I didn't take a little pleasure in seeing Wade reject her.

6

ELLIE

I had been in Atlanta over a month, and was really settling in. I decided on a school to attend and was in the process of getting registered to start next semester. Everything was falling into place, but I still hadn't met many people yet outside of the pub. The good news was I had traded a few texts with Ruthie, and we had plans to meet up for lunch later this week.

I was on the late dinner shift tonight, which started at four and went until eleven or midnight, depending on how busy we were. Tammy was on the early shift, which meant I would only get to work with her for about an hour or two tops, until Sam came in to relieve her. I liked Sam. He was young like me, but not really a chatty person, which was fine, but it certainly didn't make the shift as fun as it was with Tammy.

Most of the other staff I had met were also really cool

and great to work with, but Tammy reminded me of an older version of Katie from back home in Tennessee.

Though I guess I couldn't really call it home anymore. With Gran gone, Randall being a miserable excuse of a person, and Jack living here in Georgia now, I supposed that meant Georgia was my new home.

"Home isn't where your house is, but where your family is," Gran used to say to Jack and me shortly after we went to live with her. I used to think she only said that to make us feel better about leaving our old house behind and moving in with her, but now I was starting to get it. Georgia was where my brother lived, along with his best friends. Friends who were like brothers to him. If he was happy here, then I could be too.

I was only about an hour into my shift when Tammy came over and told me I had a phone call again. I sighed, knowing they would likely have hung up. Again.

"Watering Hole, this is Ellie," I said, but once again, I was met with silence.

"Hello? This is the Watering Hole. How can I help you?" I repeated, this time with a little more vigor.

I was just about to hang up, when a voice from my past brought chills to my body.

"Hello, Elliana. I found you," the man said slowly, saying my name in a creepy way only he could.

"Randall?" I squeaked.

"Ahhh yes, she does remember me." His voice sounded calm, but with an edge of hostility. "You can run,

Elliana, but I will always find you. You will always be mine. You. Belong. To. Me!" His voice dripped with displeasure and malice, even though it was barely above a whisper.

The room started to spin, and I had a hard time breathing. How had he found me? I knew he likely assumed I came to Georgia, but how did he track me down at work? I vaguely heard Randall's voice continue but couldn't hear what he was actually saying. I grabbed the bar to stabilize myself, and I felt the phone slide out of my hand. In my haze, I heard Tammy yell something, but all I kept thinking about was Randall had found me and he would come for me. He would never let me go.

Tammy's face came into view, and she kept telling me to take deep breaths and look at her. The scenery around me changed, but I couldn't focus on that. I needed to figure out what to do.

As my brain fog began to clear and my mind sharpened, I looked around and realized I was now sitting on the small couch in Wade's office.

"Tammy?" I asked, my voice croaking.

"There she is," she said calmly sitting in front of me. "Welcome back."

"Why am I in the office?" My voice was still barely above a whisper.

"I'm no expert, hon, but I think you had a panic

attack," she said reassuringly, though concern was etched across her face. "You were shakin' and breathin' real fast, and then you just passed out. I had Chuck come and help me carry you back here."

I'd never had a panic attack before, and I was so embarrassed that I'd had one at work. Even worse, I'd passed out and Chuck had to leave the kitchen to carry me to the office.

"I'm sorry, Tammy," I told her. "That's never happened before. I'm better now. Let me just splash some water on my face, and I'll be ready to come back out."

"Uh-uh, you're done for the night," she said sternly like a mother hen. "Sam just got here, and he's takin over the bar. Chuck is back in the kitchen. We're all set, so now I'm gonna walk you upstairs to your apartment."

"Sam is here to relieve you. My shift just started. He can't be by himself," I argued, but she held up her hand and cut me off.

"Wade's orders," she said, allowing for no counterargument. "Grab your bag, I'm gonna take you upstairs and get you settled. If Sam needs help, I'll come back down and help him out for a bit and then check on you later."

I was already embarrassed as it was, but now knowing that Wade must have heard and was pulling me off my shift, I was mortified. But Tammy was a take-charge kind of person, so I knew there was no way I would win this battle. I nodded, grabbed my purse and followed her.

She led me out the back door, giving me a little privacy from the customers seated at the bar. We walked around the side of the building to the entrance of the security and apartment lobby. Tammy followed me into my apartment and told me to sit on the couch while she got me some water. I set my purse on the kitchen counter and walked into the living room.

Tammy brought a glass of water to me and put it on the coffee table as she sat next to me on the couch.

"I don't wanna press you too much right now because you've had a rough night, but tomorrow, we're gonna talk about who was on that phone that spooked you so much," Tammy said.

I nodded and took a sip of the water. "Thanks, Tammy. For everything tonight."

"Honey, I know I may be old enough to be your mom, but us gals gotta stick together," she said, making me feel better. "You just take it easy tonight, do something that relaxes you, and I'll check in on you later."

"Okay," I said as I tried to muster up a smile.

"I know only you and the boys can get up here but lock the door after me anyway…. it'll make me feel better," she said as she gave me a small smile.

I followed her to the door; she gave me a small hug with a tight smile and left.

As I walked back to the couch, I thought about Tammy's words and decided to get out my crochet needles and yarn and keep working on the blanket I was making. My gran taught me how to crochet, and it always calmed me down.

It was still light out. I stood by the window, staring

out, my thoughts scattered. I tried to collect them, to steady myself, but the memory of the phone call sent a fresh wave of nerves through me. He had found me. He was angry. His words echoed, over and over, refusing to fade.

He would never let me go.

7

ELLIE

I woke to a light knocking on the door. Disoriented, it took me a moment to remember where I was. I must have fallen asleep on the couch. It was now dark both outside and inside my apartment. The knocking came again. Who in the world would be at my door? The only people I knew here were downstairs at work. Ah—Tammy. She must be checking on me. I started to rise from the couch to let her in, but then—scratching. My breath caught. Someone wasn't knocking anymore. Someone was trying to break in.

I didn't have time to think…I reached for my phone and realized it must still be on the kitchen counter where I'd set it when I came home. My heart was racing now as I felt around for anything to use as a weapon and my hand touched my crochet needles. Just as I grabbed the needles, my door opened. My fight-or-flight instinct kicked into gear as I realized Randall had obviously found me. I knew he wouldn't go easy on me, so I jumped from the couch toward the tall, dark figure by the door with all my strength.

"Ellie?" a voice murmured just as I lunged, crochet needle in-hand.

Oh no. No, no, no. I recognized that voice.

"Wade?" I said, my right arm still in the air.

"Yeah, it's me. What are you doing? Why don't you have any lights on?" Wade asked as he flipped the switch on with one arm and grabbed my wrist with the other.

"I, umm...didn't know it was you. Uh...sorry." I tried to get the words out, but my brain wasn't working with him touching me and being so close. He smelled woodsy with a hint of spice, and I really wanted to bury my face in his shirt and continue to smell his unique scent.

"I, uh, must have fallen asleep on the couch while it was still light out," I said, struggling with his close proximity.

"What is that?" Wade asked as he looked at my odd choice of weapon.

"It's, uh...a crochet needle," I practically whispered. "It was the best I could come up with."

"Why?" he asked, his expression blank.

"Because I crochet." I said it like that was obvious. "My gran taught me, and I like to do it because it calms me down and helps me relax," I said, a little defensive about my choice of hobby.

"I meant, why did you grab that and not your phone or a knife or something better?" he asked as he finally started to move away from me. I instantly felt sad and missed his body heat and wonderful scent.

"I think my phone is on the kitchen counter, and obviously my knives are too." I said as I moved toward the kitchen to grab my phone. "The crochet needle was the closest thing I had."

"That would explain why you didn't answer."

I looked down at my phone and sure enough, I'd had a few missed calls and texts from Wade, but I also saw a few missed calls from an unknown number. I instantly felt cold and worried it could be Randall.

"What's wrong?"

Wade was always so perceptive. I both liked it and hated it.

"Can you tell me what happened tonight?" he asked softly.

"It's a long story," I sighed.

"I've got nowhere to be," he said. Even if he did, I sensed he would have canceled those plans.

"How much did Jack tell you about our parents?" I asked.

"Not much. I know they died in a car accident and then you went to live with your grandma in Tennessee," he said with sympathy on his face.

After a long pause, I took a deep breath and told him everything.

"I always wanted to go to college, but Gran couldn't afford it. My parents left us some money when they died, but they didn't have any kind of life-insurance policy, so most of the money went to Gran so she could take care of us. I was a good student, but after my parents died and Jack left for the Army, I became depressed and struggled with school, so a scholarship wasn't going to happen. Gran did a great job caring for us, but she had my mom late in life, so she was very old and frail."

I took a deep breath to gather my courage.

"When I graduated high school, I was planning to spend that next year working as much as possible and try to apply the following year at a college nearby."

"So, the following summer, I went out with some friends, and I met Randall. He seemed really nice, charming, and had a good job working at the bank. He seemed stable and safe. We went on a few dates the next few months, and then he asked me to move in with him. I liked him, but I wasn't ready yet, so I told him no. He was the only serious boyfriend I'd ever had, but I knew deep down something felt off." I nearly groaned at how right I had been.

"I also didn't want to leave Gran all by herself. It's why I was going to go to college nearby. A few months later, I came home from my shift at the restaurant and found Gran unconscious on the floor." My voice strained as I started to get choked up. "It appears she may have had a stroke or something and fell down the s-s-stairs."

"You can take a break," Wade said calmly.

"I'm okay," I said and twisted my hands in my lap as I continued.

"Jack came home for the funeral, and he met Randall.

Jack pulled me aside at the wake and told me he thought Randall was smug and a tool, and to get rid of him. He was right, but at the time I was so emotional from Gran's death that I couldn't see it. All I could see was that everyone I loved kept leaving me, but Randall was still there. Jack left the next day to go back overseas and finish his tour, since he was only home for emergency bereavement leave."

I paused, swallowing back my emotions. Wade waited patiently for me to continue.

"After Gran died, I decided to postpone classes until the spring semester because I just couldn't handle everything that was going on. Randall moved in with me temporarily to help me out," I said, barely able to keep the disgust in my voice at bay.

I looked up at Wade and saw the silent support he was trying to give me, and it encouraged me to continue. I paused, took a breath, and looked straight into his eyes when I told him the rest.

"A few weeks later, the yelling and fighting began. He wanted me to sell Gran's house so we could buy a home together, but I wasn't ready to part with her home yet. I tried explaining this to him, and at first, he would just get angry and accuse me of not being committed to the relationship like he was, but that quickly turned to yelling and screaming and accusations of me liking other men," I said, noticing a tic in Wade's cheek, but otherwise no reaction.

"I realized at that point that I didn't want to be with

him anymore and asked him to move out. He got angry and stormed out, but then he came back and apologized —multiple times. Eventually, he moved out, though, and reluctantly bought his own place. I thought he had finally moved on for good."

I should've known it wouldn't be that easy.

"I didn't hear from him for months. During that time, Jack and I had emailed back and forth, and we decided that Gran wouldn't want us to hold on to her house, especially with all the work that needed to be done. She knew it was a money pit and would rather we spend that money on my education. I was going to come down to Georgia and stay with Jack, maybe try to find a school here. I was already registered to start school in Tennessee in a few weeks, but I figured I could try in Georgia, if I needed to.

To my surprise, Randall came by to visit me at the restaurant I worked at one night. He was back to his old charming self, and told me to sell Gran's house, move in with him, and then go to the school in Tennessee, like I always wanted. I wasn't going to, but because Gran's house sold so quickly, I figured I would just move in with Randall for a few weeks and then transition to campus housing once classes began," I explained, trying to justify it, even though I knew it sounded dumb as I said it out loud.

"I'm not judging, but did you not have any friends you could stay with?" he asked sympathetically.

"I thought about it. I really did," I sighed. "My friend Katie worked at the restaurant with me and offered to help me move in with her, but she was living in her parents' basement while she finished nursing school. The few other friends I had from high school were all away at colleges outside the state."

He nodded and sat there patiently listening while I continued.

"Two weeks after I moved in, the old Randall was back," I said quietly looking down at my hands in my lap.

"At first, he got mad at me and accused me of not appreciating his graciousness and refusing to get back together with him. I explained that I wanted to just focus on school and not get into a relationship again. Shortly after, I started having car trouble, so Randall offered to take me to and from work while my car was in the shop."

Wade's eyes hardened even further, as if he knew what was coming.

"If Katie was working, she took me to and from work since we often worked the same shift, but sometimes she had class, so Randall would do it. One of those nights, he came in a little before I left and sat at the bar. I finished up with one of my regular customers, who was a really nice guy. We talked about his newborn twins and lovely wife all the time. But apparently Randall thought there was more there. He accused me of lying to him on the car ride home. He said obviously I was interested in having a relationship with another man, just not him. I told him about the guy's wife and kids and how I was just being polite to a long-time customer."

I realized that when he was upset, there was no rationalizing with him.

"When we got home, he wouldn't drop it. He started yelling and screaming about how I was embarrassing him because he was letting me stay in his house, but I was secretly seeing other men. I started to get really angry because I was doing no such thing, and..." I paused, taking a shaky breath. I looked at Wade, and he just nodded, giving me the silent courage to keep going.

"He snapped. He slapped me across the face," I said it so quietly I wasn't sure he heard me. But the look on his face showed me he'd heard everything. His eyes were swirling with anger, and his mouth pinched into a line.

"Shocked, I stood there for a minute right after it happened, but apparently that was the wrong reaction to have, because he yelled more and pushed me up against a wall," I said slowly, noticing Wade's fists were squeezed so tight his skin was white.

"That's why you had marks on your face and neck when you first arrived here." He noted.

Both Wade and Tammy had noticed the bruises. I looked down, embarrassed for not doing a better job of covering those up. But I was also embarrassed because I knew he wouldn't like my response.

"Umm...no, not really," I said quietly, looking down at my feet. His fingers gently pushed my chin up forcing me to look at him. "No, those were from the second time."

"The *second* time?" he asked, the shock in his voice was noticeable.

I couldn't answer him or look him in the eye, so I just nodded.

"What happened, Ellie?" he asked gently.

"After he pushed me against the wall, he suddenly moved away, told me to clean myself up, and then he just left. I sat there for a few moments and then reached for my phone. I called Katie and had her come pick me up. I didn't know how long he would be gone, so I gathered a few things quickly, and stayed with Katie the next few nights. Then we made a plan for me to go back to his house when I knew he was at work and gather up the rest of my stuff. Katie and I were just going to bunk together in her parents' basement until I was ready to attend school in a few weeks."

"That's good," Wade said, giving me that little encouragement he somehow knew I needed.

"I went over the following Thursday, because I knew he usually worked late those days, so that gave me some extra cushion on the timing. Katie had to run a quick errand but was going to meet me at the house so we could load up both our cars. I went in and started packing as quickly as I could, and I heard the door open. I thought it was Katie..." My breath hitched.

Wade reached out and put his hand on top of mine which was currently digging into the top of my thigh. There was something about his touch that reassured me and made me feel stronger.

"It wasn't Katie. It was Randall. He saw me packing and started yelling. I could see the rage on his face and I tried to calm him down. He cornered me and slapped me hard across the face. He wrapped his hands around my neck and choked me. Then he...punched me, and the next thing I remember was waking up with Katie's face hovering over mine," I said, breathing hard and a little shaky.

Wade cursed, and his eyes turned menacing as he squeezed my hand. Then, as if realizing he might be squeezing too hard, he let go. I instantly missed his hand on mine.

"That's where the marks came from when you arrived here," he said, not really asking a question, just more of a confirmation.

"Yeah," I said, looking down again. "After that, I stayed with Katie for a few more days, but I realized I couldn't stay in that town any more. He knew where I worked, and even where I was planning to attend college. I emailed Jack and told him I was coming to Georgia. Once I felt good enough to drive, I got in my car and headed down here," I said.

Chancing a look up at Wade I realized he was back to the neutral face that gave away nothing.

"How much does your brother know?" he questioned.

"Just that I broke up with Randall and decided to move down here. Please don't tell him," I rushed to say. "I don't want to worry him while he's finishing up his last tour."

"You need to tell him," he said firmly.

"I wasn't planning to tell him at all, but after what happened tonight, I probably should," I sighed.

"Tammy gave me a brief synopsis, but walk me through what went down tonight at the bar."

I took a deep breath and told him about the phone calls – not just tonight, but some of the hangups that had happened the last few days. His face visibly tensed, but he nodded a few times, encouraging me as I shared details of the calls.

"Guys like your asshole ex like control," Wade said, pausing for a few moments like he was thinking about something.

My heart started racing again just thinking about Randall finding me and that he chose to escalate this.

"Did he have a security system, or any security cameras in his house?" he asked, shaking me out of my moment.

"Umm...no, no security system or cameras. Why?" I asked.

"Trying to figure out how he knew you were at his house. You said you knew he would be at work, yet he came back shortly after you arrived. Just trying to figure out why then."

"I never really thought about it. I just assumed it was bad luck on my part."

He nodded but didn't actually confirm what I was thinking.

"Go ahead and relax for a bit. I'm going to run downstairs and get some food and bring it back up," he said.

"You don't have to do that. I'm fine," I protested, shaking my head.

"Non-negotiable," he insisted. "I'm going to get food, we're going to eat, and then we're going to talk about some new security measures for you at work." Then he turned and walked out the door before I had a chance to respond.

That man both infuriated me and drew me in at the same time. He was kind, but bossy, and I wasn't sure how I felt about it.

8

WADE

I left Ellie's apartment and immediately went down to the kitchen and asked Chuck to make me a burger and whatever Ellie usually ate.

"Yeah, man. I'll make her favorite," he replied, then paused, leaning against the counter. "Tammy gave me the lowdown on the phone call. She doin' okay now?"

His concern for her only confirmed what I already knew—Ellie had a way of worming her way into people's hearts, even in the short time she'd been here.

"She's still a bit shaken up, but better," I responded, trying to ease his concerns.

Chuck wiped his hands on a towel and gave me a serious look. "You need my help sending this asshole a message?" he asked, his voice low and steady. "She's a sweet girl. She don't need nobody hassling her."

I told him I had it handled for now and that seemed to satisfy him for the moment. After getting the food order squared away, I went into my office and called Archer. We had cameras all over the building, but I wanted to put a few more security measures in place. With pricks like Randall, they often escalated once they felt they'd lost control over a situation. My guess was he was pissed Ellie left and was making his move to scare her. If he was dumb enough to stalk her here, I wanted to be prepared. I also wanted to see if we could trace some of those phone calls made to the Watering Hole. Archer said he and Vince would look into it and see what they could find.

Something also wasn't sitting well with me about his perfectly timed arrival at his house when Ellie was packing up. Or how he'd found her at this pub. I also asked Vince what to do about Jack. I understood Ellie didn't want to worry him, but Archer and I both agreed he should know and would be pissed if he found out we'd kept it from him. Plus, he'd met the prick, albeit briefly, so he may be able to shed some light into his behavior. I rattled off an email to Jack to have him give me a call when he could, knowing it could be days before he was able to.

Just the thought of this dickhead messing with Ellie had my blood boiling. When she'd told me what he'd done to her, it took everything in me to remain calm for her sake. Any man who can do that to a woman or child is not a man and, in my opinion, doesn't deserve to share space on this Earth.

While I waited for the food, I went in search of Tammy to fill her in on a few things. While Tammy had worked here for years with my uncle, what many people didn't know was that she was also former military and a badass in her own right. While she never outright lied about her military past if people asked, she also didn't share her exact role freely. She said that if she ever felt the need to bring those skills back again, she liked having the advantage and element of surprise of people not knowing she could kick someone's ass if she needed to.

"Hey Tammy, you got a minute?" I asked after spotting her near the bar. I knew she'd called in extra help for the bar so she wouldn't have to work too long.

"Yeah, Corey just got here, so give me a minute and I'll meet ya back in the office," she said, nodding toward the back.

I walked back, telling Chuck I'd come get the food in a few minutes, and then made my way to the office. Tammy came in about a minute later.

"Normally I don't like going behind people's backs, but I need to know what's going on with Ellie, so spill," she said sternly with her arms crossed leaning against the doorway.

"Have a seat." I pointed to the chair in front of me.

She closed the door and sat.

"It's not my story to tell, but the gist of it is that Ellie has an abusive ex, and while she left him and came here, it appears he somehow found her," I explained, giving her the bare minimum but also the essentials she needed.

"When you say abusive, we talkin' emotional, verbal, or physical?" Tammy asked.

"Definitely the last two, but likely all the above," I told her and could see her face tighten and breathing pick up. "Dipshit's name is Randall. I got Archer and Vince looking into him as we speak, but definitely let me know if you see or hear anything around here. Not sure how he found out she's working here, but he knows now."

"He knows her brother works with you guys upstairs? Could be a guess?" Tammy asked.

"I thought that too, but it appeared that while she mentioned her brother living here in town while he wasn't overseas, she hadn't given him any specifics of *where* he lived, and she didn't even know we had Ranger Shield up and running yet, so I doubt she gave that asshole anything he could use to find us."

I told Tammy if that guy or anyone else called back asking for Ellie specifically, to let me know right away. She confirmed and told me she would let me know if she heard or saw anything.

I grabbed our food from Chuck and made my way back upstairs.

Once upstairs, I knocked at her door. I had a key to unlock it, but didn't want to startle her, plus my hands were full of food.

Ellie opened it, but I hadn't heard her unlock it.

"You should keep this locked at all times," I told her as I walked into the kitchen.

"You said you were coming right back, and you already told me you guys keep this building very secure."

"Yes, we do. It's very secure, but now that your ex-douche canoe knows where you work, and you live where you work, you shouldn't take any chances," I explained to her so she understood the importance.

Her smile dropped, and I instantly felt bad.

"Okay, sorry," she said in a more somber voice.

"Let's eat," I said, holding up the bags and setting things up at the two barstools Jack had in his apartment in lieu of an actual table and chairs.

I felt bad bringing the mood down, so I tried to think of something else to talk about to get her mind off it, though I wasn't exactly great at mindless small talk.

"What was Jack like as a kid? Got any embarrassing stories you wanna share that we can give him hell for when he comes back?" I asked.

She laughed and her smile instantly reappeared, making me feel good about my choice of conversation.

"Did he ever tell you about the time he got his braces stuck on a girl's braces while making out with her—then had to go to her dad to get them unstuck?" She giggled, a definite devious edge in her voice. It was contagious—I laughed, too.

"No, can't say he did. Do tell," I urged, prying for more.

She launched into three more gloriously embarrassing stories, giving me plenty of details to share with the other guys so we could properly give Jack a hard time later.

"What about you? Do you have any siblings?" she asked me.

"I have one older sister, Willa," I told her. "She and her husband Paul live here in Georgia, and they have two kids, Charlie who's nine, and Haley who's seven. I also have a younger sister Whitney, who is going to college here in Georgia. She's training to be a vet, so she only has one year left of her forty-seven years of vet school."

"Oh, that's awesome," she said, laughing a little. God her face was beautiful when she laughed freely like that.

"What about your parents? Do they live here too?" she asked with a smile still on her face.

"Yeah, they still live in the same house I grew up in," I explained, feeling a bit lucky knowing she didn't have her parents anymore. "They all get together with my grandma, who also lives nearby, every Sunday for lunch or dinner. I can't usually go because of my schedule at the pub, but I try to go once a month or so if I can."

Her smile on her face now turned sad, and I couldn't help but feel bad that she didn't have that anymore, given both her parents and her grandma were dead. My family annoyed the hell out of me at times, but I still loved having them here, and holidays were great. Chaotic, but great.

"I miss that," she sighed. "We used to do family dinners too, though my grandma lived a little farther away. Jack is all I have left, but he's gone so much, I don't really get to see him often. God, I miss him."

She started to choke up a little, and I felt this tightening in my chest. I felt so bad for her, which was the only reason I could imagine why I did what I did next.

"Why don't you come with me tomorrow to family dinner?" I asked. "It's nothing fancy. It will be crazy and loud, but the food is great."

"You sure they won't mind?" she asked a little anxiously. "I don't want to intrude."

"You're not intruding," I said. "My mom and grandma will be thrilled to have someone else, though I warn you, I don't make it a habit of bringing anyone with me, so I'm sure my sisters will fill you with embarrassing stories from my childhood too."

She smiled again, and her face lit up.

"Oooh, that could be fun." She grinned that slightly devious grin again, and I wanted to kiss that right off her face.

Stop that thought.

You're already close to crossing the line, inviting her to see your family.

Lord knew Mom, Grandma, Whitney, and Willa will have a field day with me bringing home a woman. Something I had never ever done.

"Thank you," she said, bringing me back from my thoughts. "I actually wouldn't mind meeting your mom. Jack said she used to send the best care packages and would often add in things for the other guys too. I tried, but after Gran died, I was so overcome with grief that I stopped sending stuff as regularly as I used to."

"Don't worry about it. My mom took it upon herself to

adopt all ten guys in our squadron and basically become our den mom," I told her.

It was true. My mom sent stuff for me and the other guys, especially the ones like Jack and a few others who didn't have parents or other family to send care packages to them.

"What's your mom's name?" she asked.

"Her name is Wendy, and my father's name is Wayne," I told her, adding in my dad's name, knowing full well what she would ask afterward.

"You all have names starting with W, and isn't your last name Watson?" She grinned. "Was that on purpose?"

I sighed and rolled my eyes.

"Yes, Mom thought it was cute," I explained. "I'm pretty sure my dad thought it was weird, but he told her since she was the one giving birth, she could pick the names."

I was pretty sure my dad regretted that, but if he did, he would take that thought to his grave rather than upset my mom.

"It's a sore subject with her and my sister Willa since she decided not to continue the trend with her kids," I told her.

"But her husband's name doesn't start with a W," she intelligently pointed out.

"Yep, but that didn't mean anything to my mom," I said. "And even though Willa's kids are older now and clearly aren't going to have their names changed, my mother still brings it up at least once a year at family get-togethers."

She laughed, and I swore I felt that in my dick. God, she looked so gorgeous when she laughed.

Maybe it was the situation earlier in the day, or maybe it was how relaxed I felt with her, or maybe it was just the fact that she looked so damn beautiful at this moment while laughing, but my brain obviously malfunctioned, because I leaned forward and kissed her. Hard. I wrapped my hand around the back of her neck and pulled her closer to me. Holy hell, she tasted good.

For the first couple seconds, she was stiff, but then she tilted her head and kissed me right back, opening her mouth to me. I slipped my tongue in there and tasted her some more. Desire filled me with an urgency that kept all logical thought at bay. She moaned, and that sound went straight to my dick, which was now hard as a rock. That moan also woke my brain right up.

Get off her. I pulled away quickly and backed away from her.

"Jesus, I'm sorry," I said, instantly regretting losing her mouth but also regretting my impulse control. I needed to leave now before I did it again.

Without giving her any chance to say anything, I made my way to the door.

"I'll come get you at noon tomorrow for lunch," I said as I opened the door and walked out. I walked right over to my door and let myself out.

I needed to get control of myself around her. In a

matter of minutes, I'd invited her to my family lunch and had my tongue down her throat. *What the hell were you thinking?*

Never in my life had I craved someone like I craved Ellie. It was like I was a teenage boy all over again with no impulse control around girls.

That stops now, before you make an even bigger mistake. Oh, and Jack kills you for touching his sister.

9

ELLIE

What the hell just happened?

One minute I was laughing; the next Wade's mouth was on mine, giving me the best kiss of my entire life. God, that man could kiss. I didn't have much experience outside of Randall, since during my peak teenage years my parents died, I moved to a new state with my grandma and started a new school, then my brother left, and I helped pick up more of the workload around the house with Gran.

I wasn't upset about my limited experience. It was just that I didn't know whether Randall was just not that great of a kisser or if Wade was just that amazing.

All I knew was that I loved the feel of his beard – it both tickled and scratched my face, and oddly I loved it. When he stuck his tongue in my mouth, I felt something short-circuit in my brain. My insides warmed just at the memory of that kiss. I could have spent hours kissing Wade, but alas, that was part of the problem.

Getting involved with another man so soon after Randall was a bad idea, even if that man was nothing like him. I knew from my conversations with Tammy and the others at the pub as well as my brother that Wade was nothing like Randall. Sure, Randall had friends, but he didn't treat them the same way that Wade did. If one of his friends or co-workers needed him, Wade would do everything in his power to help, and I knew from my brother that Wade had put Jack's life before his while they were overseas.

Jack would never get specific about any of his missions or locations, but he'd mentioned multiple times that Wade had saved his life by tackling him to the ground right before a sniper would have hit and killed him. Randall would never risk his life to save another, not even his own family. One of many red flags I didn't see until it was too late.

Wade was a good man through and through. That still didn't mean it would be a good decision to get involved with him. But Wade was the kind of man who made that kind of decision really hard. He smelled so good too, and when he grabbed my face...*Sigh*. His kiss was rough, but his hands grabbed my face gently, as though he was caressing me and soaking it in, yet some part of him lost control and he couldn't get enough. I totally understood that. I'd felt the same, and then he'd ended it. Abruptly.

He'd even apologized. I wasn't sure if that was because he regretted kissing me or he thought I did.

Maybe he'd thought it inappropriate since he was my boss, or maybe because of what happened earlier in the day. And, yes, admittedly, it was a rough day, which brought me back to my original thought of how dumb I was for falling for Randall and staying with him longer than I should have. Why couldn't I have found a man like Wade, instead of a crazy person like Randall?

God...Randall. How had he even found me? I'd told him I was coming to Georgia, but I'd never mentioned where Jack lived. I'd never mentioned the new security company he was setting up with his friends, since Jack never really told me much about that to begin with. Randall never seemed interested in wanting to visit my brother or even get to know him. I realized now that should have been yet another red flag. So many red flags.

My phone buzzed next to me, and I saw it was a text from Ruthie.

> Hey Ellie, it's Ruthie. I hope you don't mind, but Archer told me what happened tonight at the pub. I'm so sorry.

Great. I sighed and leaned my head back to look at the ceiling. Wade must have alerted everyone at Ranger Shield about what had happened, including Ruthie. This was so embarrassing. Another message pinged on my phone, and I looked down.

RUTHIE:

I take self-defense classes two nights a week. You can totally say no, but you're welcome to come with me if you want.

While it was embarrassing that word of tonight's incident was spreading, it was also really sweet of her to reach out—especially since, on the surface, she seemed like an introvert. Besides, I'd always thought about taking a self-defense class but never actually looked into it. Maybe this was a sign to finally do it.

ME:

Hey Ruthie, I would love to. Thanks for inviting me. Just let me know when the next class is, and I would love to come.

We made a plan to meet Tuesday morning to go before we both had to be at work.

I decided to just go to bed and start fresh the next day. I could pick Wade's brain about Randall tomorrow on the way to his family's house.

Oh God. There went the anxiety-meter again. I was going to meet his family. I didn't know why I was suddenly so nervous about that. It wasn't like we were together, and I was meeting *my* future family.

Oh, but that kiss. I put my fingers to my lips and could still feel his lips on mine. Would his family know we kissed? I shook my head. *Don't be ridiculous*, I thought. Just be yourself, and go there to enjoy a home-cooked meal and meet Wade's family. This is Jack's best friend.

You are meeting his best friend's family. That's how we approach this.

At least, that was how I convinced myself I would treat this lunch tomorrow. The sister of Wade's best friend.

As I climbed into my bed, I tried to calm my brain from all that had happened today. No sense stressing about meeting Wade's family or Randall finding me any more tonight when my brain was officially fried.

Remember what Gran used to say. *Focus on the positives and things I can control.*

I was finally starting to make friends.

I enjoyed my job.

I was going to start school soon and finally accomplish that goal on my list.

I was really excited for this new chapter of my life— my new beginning.

10

WADE

I finally gave up on getting any decent sleep around five a.m., after a night of tossing and turning. I'd like to blame it all on dealing with Ellie's piece-of-shit ex, but that wouldn't be the whole truth. The kiss had crept into my thoughts, too. More than a few times.

When I walked back into my apartment last night, my dick was as hard as it'd ever been. Normally, I would just go seek out one of the women I had been with in the past who might be amenable to meeting up occasionally to mutually scratch that itch, but none of them appealed to my dick. Nope, that appendage wanted Ellie, and Ellie only.

Well, shit.

My only option was to take myself in hand in the shower, but that felt just as wrong as being with her in real life. Still, unless I wanted to have a hard-on at the family lunch later today, I had no choice. Just this once, I let myself fantasize about what she would feel like. Her curves, her soft hair, that supple ass.

If she hadn't moaned loudly last night, waking my brain back to reality I may have taken things too far with her, and I couldn't do that.

I liked women. Immensely. But ever since my military training, I had never lost control around one. Fantasies may come to mind, but I could compartmentalize and shut that down, change my focus if I needed to. Not with Ellie. That woman was like a powerful drug I could not break free from. She was addictive.

Now, because I was an idiot, I would be spending much of the day with her and my family. Together.

What could possibly go wrong?

I internally groaned, knowing my family would jump on the fact that Ellie was the first woman I'd brought home in a very long time, and they would pounce on the ability to share embarrassing stories about me.

Since sleep was not going to come for me, I decided to get up and work off the frustration in the gym. I also called Archer and Vince to give them some more details and thoughts I had on Ellie's stalker. Vince was going to head to the bar and put caller ID and a recorder on the phone just in case he called again. We decided we would touch base tomorrow morning at the office and look into a few other things.

I worked out, showered, and threw in a load of laundry, and I was about to walk over and get Ellie when there was a knock on my door. I opened it to find Ellie standing there looking beautiful in a colorful summer dress. Thin yellow straps showed off how tan her shoulders were. It was tight through her top and then flowed down to her knees. And it was very apparent she was not wearing a bra underneath.

Jeez, she was going to kill me today. So much for trying to rub one out in the shower to make sure I didn't have an erection at the family lunch.

"Hey, I didn't have much time, and I wasn't sure what your family was serving, so I just threw together a small side dish. Hopefully, that's okay," she said, holding out a glass container I hadn't noticed since I was too preoccupied with looking at her.

"You don't need to bring anything, Ellie," I told her because I certainly never did.

"I most certainly do!" she said, and I just nodded because, having my sisters, mother, and grandmother around most of my childhood, I knew better than to argue with a woman about food.

We walked out to the car, and I was glad she walked behind me, so I didn't embarrass myself by staring at her ass the whole time. I needed to regain my focus here, or my family would start asking too many questions. Questions I wasn't even ready to answer myself.

I used the car ride to explain to her that my family was a lot, and she should be prepared for them to be in her space and annoy her with questions. I even gave her a few examples of how nosy the women in my family could be. She just smiled and took it in stride, saying she didn't mind. I hope she still felt that way when we left.

At least I'd warned her.

We pulled up the long drive to the house and I could see my sister Willa, Paul, and their kids all on the big wraparound front porch. Well, this was about to get exciting real fast.

"I'll get out first and come around and let you out of your door," I told her as I shut off the engine.

"I appreciate the chivalry Wade, but I can open my own door," she responded with a chuckle.

"Yes, you can, but if you do, those mini humans over there will likely jump all over you, and trust me, they can be feral," I explained, pointing at my niece and nephew. "Sit tight. I'll come around."

She laughed but thankfully waited in the car for me. As I rounded the car, I saw my niece and nephew come running off the front porch towards me. I slowly opened Ellie's door to see her smirking at me as though she thought I was the funny one. Whatever. I tried to warn her.

I glanced back up to see my niece and nephew edging closer but also saw the gleam of surprise in my sister's eyes just before she hopped up and yelled back into the house at the top of her lungs, "Mom! Quick! Wade brought a girl!" Willa clapped her hands excitedly.

Before I had time to really think about that, two little barbarians jumped on me.

"Uncle Wade! Uncle Wade you're here!" they both squealed.

I saw the moment they realized there was another person. They didn't let go of me but stared at Ellie like she was an alien. I figured it would be best to make quick introductions before my mom and sister made their way over.

"This tall monster is Charlie." I pointed at my nephew on my right. "And the mermaid is Haley," I explained to Ellie while pointing at the mermaid costume my niece was currently wearing.

"Guys, this is Ellie," I said, pointing beside me.

"Are you Wade's girlfriend?" Charlie asked, but before Ellie even had a chance to answer, Haley decided to interrupt with her own comments and questions.

"You're very pretty," she said. "Do you like mermaids? You look like a mermaid. Do you want to wear a mermaid tail?" She said the entire thing without taking a breath between questions.

Ellie just giggled and smiled beside me.

"Alright, hooligans. Calm down. Can we at least let Ellie get inside to the kitchen so she can drop off the food?" I asked while they both still held on to my arms. Trying to pull away from them slightly, I felt my sister come up to us.

"I'll help with the food. Hello! I'm Willa," my sister interrupted, sticking her hand between Ellie and me and slowly squeezed her way in. "Kids," my sister said conspiratorially. "Uncle Wade is just *dying* to see your new pet. Why don't you take him inside and show him," she said as the kids screamed and grabbed my arms, yanking me toward the house away from Ellie.

"Hey, everybody, let me get Ellie inside first please," I tried to explain as the kids kept pulling me away from Ellie and my sister kept encroaching closer to her.

"Don't worry, I'll take good care of her!" Willa yelled, waving me off.

Yeah. That's what I was worried about.

God only knew what she would be telling her while I was gone. My niece and nephew continued to pull my arms, guiding me up the steps into the house.

I passed my brother-in-law, still sitting on the front porch like nothing was at all out of the ordinary. That or maybe he just became immune to the chaos. He did that head lift acknowledgment that men often did as I was dragged by his kids into my parents' house.

"Hi sweetheart. I'm so glad you could make it," I heard my mom say to me as she appeared in the door-way. I tried to hug her and use it as my way to escape the clutches of the two kids attached to me, but no such luck.

"We're taking Uncle Wade to see Snickers!" Haley told my mom.

"Oh well, then go right ahead, dear. But please bring Uncle Wade back to the kitchen when you're done so I can put him to work," my mom said, winking at me.

I had no idea what Snickers was, but I had a feeling my mother was enjoying this.

"We will!" both kids yelled as they pulled me farther into the house and toward the living room.

Sitting on the coffee table was a cage with what appeared to be a mouse.

"Meet Snickers, our new pet hamster!" Charlie said. "Isn't he so cool?"

"Definitely," I told them while lying straight to their faces.

"When did you get this?" I asked, because I could have sworn my sister told me no pets until they were older because she didn't want to get stuck taking care of it by herself.

"We got it from our neighbor," Haley started to explain. "Charlie and me were outside playing in the yard and the guy gived it to us for free because he was moving. Isn't that awesome?"

I grinned and nodded because I was sure my sister and Paul were thrilled with their former neighbor just gifting their kids a free pet with no advance notice. They showed me the cage and setup they had for Snickers while also explaining all the cool things he could do. If I'd let them, they would have kept talking about Snickers and showing me things for an hour, so I used my mother's excuse and told them I had to go find Grandma in the kitchen and help her before she got mad. They nodded and waved me off, moving their attention back to Snickers.

As I was walking back toward the kitchen, I heard several female voices laughing and rolled my eyes. Whatever conversation was happening likely was about me, and if my sisters were in there, it was highly plausible it was embarrassing. Getting closer, I slowed up so I could listen just outside the room off to the side and out of view.

"When you say clumsy child, what do you mean?" Ellie asked innocently enough, and I knew they were absolutely talking about me. I was very much a klutz as a kid and had terrible coordination until my late teen years.

"Like a bull in a China shop, full-blown klutz," my sister Whitney enthusiastically answered. "So, Mom put him in ballet and gymnastics classes with me to help him."

"He gave me his allowance every week for three months so I wouldn't tell his friends," Willa laughed.

I rolled my eyes, remembering how I practically begged her not to tell my friends initially, until it worked out in my favor.

"I still can't believe you did that to your poor brother," my mom chided my sister. "Though a few months into it, he realized all the other girls loved having a cute boy in class."

This was true and the main reason why I stuck with it. It helped me with my coordination and set me up with my first kiss. A girl named Heather from my ballet class. Also, my second kiss with Bridget, and third kiss with Stephanie from gymnastics.

I chose that moment to walk in and interrupt my sisters, who were no doubt getting ready to embarrass me more.

"When I told my friends how many girls I got to make

out with after class they all wanted to sign up a week later, so it worked out for me," I said, flashing a sly grin at my sisters.

"You are such a sleazy braggart," Willa said, sticking out her tongue.

"Children!" my mother said, chiding us like we were little kids again. "Quit acting like you are five years old in front of our guest. She's going to think I raised you this awful on purpose."

I heard Ellie chuckle as my sister and I both rolled our eyes. Normally my mom wouldn't care, but I knew she was trying to impress Ellie while also trying to learn everything about her to see if she would be great wife material to give her more future grandkids. I closed my eyes and shook my head.

"Get your handsome face over here and hug your grandma before I die of old age and never get to see you again," said my grandma, who had been sitting quietly enjoying the show from the side of the kitchen island.

"Hey, Nana. How're you doing?" I asked, walking over to her and giving her a hug and kiss on the cheek.

"Better now that my whole family is here," she said, smiling.

I knew she meant it politely, but it also made me feel a little guilty because I was often the holdout for these gatherings.

"What am I? Chopped liver?" Whitney asked from beside her.

I leaned over and grabbed her and squeezed her hard

until she begged me to let her go while laughing. I did, but not before rubbing my hand over the top of her head and messing with her hair, causing her to growl at me as I walked back over toward the kitchen island.

"You told Willa's mini-spawns you needed my help, Ma, so what can I do?" I asked my mom, who was still getting all the food together.

"Your sisters and I have it covered for now, but when the rolls come out of the oven, I'll have you start carrying things into the table," she said, pointing at several bowls already laid out on the kitchen island. Man, it smelled good. My mom was a great cook, and so was my grandma, though she mostly just supervised nowadays since her arthritis was bad. Usually, she just gave my mom a hard time, telling her how she was cooking stuff wrong just to get on her nerves.

Just then my niece and nephew came into the kitchen with their hamster in their hands.

"Ah ah ah, *no* hamsters in my kitchen!" my mom said, shooing them out.

"But Grandma, we wanna show Wade's girlfriend our new pet!" they whined.

"Then you can do it in the living room where I don't have to worry about Snickers leaving *presents* in my kitchen," she told them.

They both looked up at Ellie and pleaded with her to come with them.

"Sure, I would love to." She smiled as she followed them out of the kitchen.

She was gone no more than five seconds before all the female members of my family pounced.

"She seems very nice. How long have you two been dating and not telling me?" my mom asked in a sweet voice but with definite cheeky undertones.

"She's good with the kids. You should marry her quickly so I can get some more great-grandbabies before I die soon," my grandmother added.

I scoffed dramatically as I replied back to her with just as much attitude as she gave me.

"Nana, you're going to live to be 120 just to spite all of us. You've got plenty more time on this Earth to give us all hell, so quit meddling." I shot her a knowing look, and she stared right back at me with a calculated smile.

"I don't meddle, young boy. I use years of wisdom to come up with impeccable ideas and execute them to perfection." She smirked right back at me, full of sass as usual.

I laughed, first because she still called me young boy, even though I was nearly thirty and almost twice her size, and second because she'd always been witty to a fault, and I loved her for it.

"She told us you work together at the bar, and she lives right next door to you...How convenient," Willa interjected with an evil smirk.

I knew she was trying to stir the pot too, but I wasn't going to take the bait.

"Yes, we do work together," I said, giving her the bare minimum.

"She said her brother was in your little group of Army friends too," my mother commented, which made me chuckle at how she labeled the guys in my squadron, as though it was just a little boys club who hung out overseas, playing cards and passing the time.

"Yeah, her brother is Jack," I confirmed to my mom, who no doubt knew which one he was since she always asked about all of them and even sent extra stuff for each of them when she would send me a care package.

"Oh, he's the one who lost his parents and grandmother, yes?" she asked, pausing what she was doing with a sad look on her face.

I wasn't surprised she remembered because that was my mom. She was great at remembering all the details about people.

I nodded at her but felt the need to change the subject because I didn't want Ellie walking back in here and thinking we were talking about her family behind her back.

"Where is Dad?" I asked, realizing he was nowhere to be found.

"I'll allow that diversion, only because I need you to get him," my mom explained. "He's outside tinkering in his garden again. I asked him to grab a few more tomatoes for the salad, but that was thirty minutes ago. Why don't you go grab him and bring him in. Food's almost ready anyway."

I wasn't going to waste an opportunity to get away from this fierce interrogation, so I made my way outside, looking for my dad. My mom was right. He was crouched down pruning some of his various vegetable plants when I walked up beside him.

"Hey Dad. Mom said you were out here *tinkering* in your garden and I'm to collect you and bring you in for lunch," I said with a grin, knowing my mom's words would get to him.

"Ugh." He sighed shaking his head. "Men do not tinker. I swear your mom said that just to annoy me."

I laughed, enjoying nettling him on purpose too.

"Good to see you, son," he said as he got up and brushed the dirt off his hands before coming around to put his hand on my shoulder and clap my back. "Never know whether to expect you for these things since you've got the new business."

I knew he didn't mean it in a rude way, so I tried not to take offense to his comment.

"Yeah, it's been busy, but I should come more often. Sorry," I muttered.

"No need to apologize. I get it," he sympathized. "It's tough getting a business up and running from scratch."

I nodded as he handed me a handful of tomatoes from the garden.

"Take those in and add them to your mom's salad, I'm going to go change my shirt since I got dirt all over it fixing my babies."

I smiled at my dad's use of the term babies for his garden. He'd struggled at first with retirement, but this garden project really gave him something to do, and he enjoyed the fruits of his labor being used for my mom's cooking.

As I walked back into the kitchen my mom was the only one in there, and she was carrying a dish in her hands.

"Oh good. Rinse those and put them right in the salad on the counter and then please bring it out to the dining room table," my mom said. "We're ready to eat."

I did what she asked and realized my mistake the moment I walked into the dining room seeing my niece and nephew sitting on either side of Ellie, which meant I would have to sit across from her. I sat down, looking over at her to hear my nephew rambling on and on about Minecraft. I highly doubted Ellie knew about anything he was talking about, but she sat there and gave him her full attention while he talked about creepers and endermen in great detail.

She was good with kids and would make a great mother someday. A tinge of pain in my chest hit me at the realization that for that to happen, she would have to be with another man, and I hated that that thought bothered me.

My dad and brother-in-law sat on either side of me and asked me about the security business. Every once and in a while, I would look up and see Ellie staring at me and listening to what I was saying. I was sure she was curious since her brother would be working for us too when he came home.

After we finished the meal, the banter between

everyone was good, and I realized how well Ellie fit right in with everyone. It made me want to make more of an effort to be here, though I'd want Ellie to be here too, and that made me pause since my family would certainly get the wrong idea if I kept bringing her back every meal.

As we finished up, Charlie begged Ellie to come see his Minecraft card collection, which she agreed to, likely under obligation and duress.

Haley informed the rest of us that we must come see the unicorn section of the garden my dad made her. We all walked outside to the backyard to check it out.

As we were listening to Haley's entertaining explanation about how unicorns are the best and they need a special section of the garden just for themselves, I felt my phone ring in my pocket and saw it was Tammy calling. Great. Someone had likely called in sick, and she was calling to ask me what to do.

"Hey Tammy," I said.

"Hey, boss-man. Everything is good here, but you said you wanted me to let you know if that man called again for Ellie," she said.

I ground my teeth, feeling my anger rise.

"I did what you said and told him she no longer worked here," she said in a somber voice. "At first, I wasn't sure he believed me, but when I added a few details to try to make it more believable, he seemed to get angry."

That wasn't a good sign that he was that quick to

anger when he didn't get what he wanted, though if it really was Ellie's ex, that wouldn't surprise me.

"You sure it's the same guy?" I asked.

"If it's the same one that called the other day when I picked up, then yes, it's the same voice," she confirmed. "It happened about seven minutes ago, and I know Vince was by earlier to install some fancy stuff on the phone here to track him, so I just wanted to let you know."

She was right. After I talked with the guys last night, Vince came over to the pub this morning to install caller ID and a few other things Tammy didn't need to know about.

"Do you want me to call her and find out where she is? Make sure she's safe?" she asked, and I appreciated her concern for Ellie.

"She's with me," I said simply. There was a pause before she spoke again, full-fledged amusement in her voice.

"Innnnnnnnteresting," Tammy teased.

"I just brought her to my parents' for lunch to keep an eye on her, so don't start," I tried to explain, but it was no use with her.

"The weekly family lunch that you never seem to find time to go to, but now you magically make time in order to take Ellie to? Veeeeeeeeery interesting," she added, leaning into it even more.

"I'm hanging up now. Call me if anything else happens," I told her as I hung up the phone. Then I shot a quick text off to Vince to let him know about the call. No sooner had I put the phone back in my pocket, both my sisters came right up next to me.

"Who pooped in your cornflakes?" Whitney asked me. "Your face looks like you want to murder someone." my sister added jokingly. If only she knew.

"The correct phrase is who pissed in your Cheerios," I informed her.

She waved her hands, practically dismissing me.

"Whatever," she said and then leaned in conspiratorially in a loud whisper. "So, who are we murdering today?"

"No one," I told them.

"Does it have something to do with the pretty blonde you brought to the family gathering today, which you *never* do," Willa said, looking at me with an accusatory face but also a full smile.

"She's a co-worker and Jack's little sister," I defended.

"I may not be good at getting phrases or memes correct, but I'm not stupid," Whitney said. "And Willa is right. You haven't stopped staring at her for more than ten seconds since you've been here."

"I don't spend that much time staring at *my* co-workers," Willa said.

That was because I couldn't stop thinking about the kiss every time I looked at her. I needed to steer them away from this topic of conversation.

"That's because you're married," I interjected. "Speaking of co-workers, got anybody you could recommend for me for our security business?"

"I'm only allowing you to deflect the conversation for

now, because, yes, I do in fact have some recommenda-tions," Willa answered. "Guy named Dane Enderson. He interviewed for our security position, but he is actually overqualified for what we need for this entry-level job. I'll send you his info in an email. I also have another guy you should reach out to. I really shouldn't be recom-mending him because he currently works for us, and he's great."

That had my attention. Why would she try to pass off someone who was supposedly good at their current job, unless there was something wrong?

"What's the catch?" I asked.

"His name is Axel Skarsgård, and he is great at his job, truly, but he looks miserable sitting at a desk all day," she explained. "He was in the Swedish military before coming to the U.S. and taking this job. Dude looks like a Viking and barely fits in his cubicle. Any time we do projects off-site or even outdoors, he looks like he just won the lottery. I just think he might be a better fit for you than us."

She turned to me and pointed her finger in my face. "But if you tell anyone I gave his information to you I will kill you."

That made me smile. My sister couldn't hurt a fly if she tried, let alone a human, but I would humor her.

"Your warning is crystal clear, sis. And thanks, for both recommendations."

She nodded like she was proud of herself for helping solve world peace.

"Back to more important topics," Whitney said while

rubbing her hands together no doubt plotting evil things. "I like her. Ellie, I mean. She seems to be good for you."

I sighed, not wanting to entertain this topic at all. I practically growled her name low to send a warning to drop it.

"Your growls don't scare me, little brother," Willa said, waving me off. "Look, I know that woman you dated, and I use that term loosely, messed you up." Her mouth looked like she'd bitten into a lemon. "But Candace didn't deserve you."

I tried to interrupt and defend Candace because no woman should have to put up with what I did to her, but Willa just kept right on talking.

"Uh-uh, no, I'm gonna stop you right there." Willa held up her hand in my face. "You would never hurt that woman on purpose. It was only ever in your sleep, and instead of trying to get you help with your nightmares, she ran away."

"It's not that simple," I tried to explain. I regretted the one time I got drunk and confided in her husband, because he obviously told Willa everything.

"Fair, but she also never tried," she said, sensing my rising anger. "Look, I'm done bringing her up. All I'm saying is don't let Candace prevent you from opening yourself up to someone else... whether that's Ellie or another woman."

I heard what she was saying, but I just couldn't do that to a woman. Especially someone like Ellie. Even if she wasn't Jack's sister and my employee, she had already been in one abusive relationship. Being with me, when I could inadvertently hurt her in my sleep, would only add to her trauma, and I couldn't do that.

"Okay," she said, clapping her hands. "Done with big sister talk. Now, you better go over there and rescue that girl from Mom and Nana."

I looked over and sighed. They had photo albums pulled out from my childhood, regaling her with even more embarrassing stories.

"Don't worry. I already told her most of your embarrassing childhood stories. There's not much left for them to tell," she said, giving me a huge fake smile.

"Are you always such a smartass?"

"No, thank you very much. Sometimes I'm sleeping," she said as she stuck out her tongue and walked away.

I walked over to collect Ellie and head out. When I got close, I heard my mom and grandma talking about the pub, and Ellie invited them to come for a meal. Great. More opportunities for them to meddle.

I told them Tammy called and we needed to head back to the pub so I could get a few things taken care of. Ellie looked at me funny like she knew I wasn't saying everything, but she didn't call me out on it, and I appreciated it. We said goodbye to all the family, and my mom brought over some leftovers for us to take back with us.

The walk back to the car was quiet, which was good for me since I was going through how to handle the call Tammy took at the pub. I was happy Ellie waited until we got inside the car to say anything.

"I like listening to you talk about the security business," she said, which was not the topic I thought she would bring up, but this was a safer topic, so I went with it.

"So, you know what your brother will be doing?" I asked as I drove us back to our building.

"Well, yes, but also, you have so much pride in your voice when you talk about it," she explained. "You seem genuinely excited about it, and that joy is contagious, I guess."

I was excited, but I guess I just never realized my excitement was that obvious.

"Yeah, so far it's doing well, and we're picking up clients, which means we need to hire some extra people sooner rather than later," I told her, as I mentioned that my sister might have some people in mind.

We talked about the business and what role her brother might take on when he got back to the States. She seemed genuinely curious, and I enjoyed talking with her about it.

"What did Tammy call about?" she asked.

I chuckled, wondering how she'd waited that long to bring that up.

"How long have you been sitting there thinking about that?" I asked.

"I was trying not to because I figured you would tell me if I needed to know, but I'm not the most patient person and couldn't help myself," she said, blushing and honestly looking a bit chagrined.

As much as I didn't want to worry her, she needed to know. Especially since I had decided right after the call with Tammy that she would not be staying in her apartment alone tonight. Not until I could talk to Archer and Vince tomorrow and add a few extra security cameras.

"Tammy called to let me know that you had another mystery caller today," I said cautiously while trying to look at her and the road at the same time to see her reaction. I didn't want her to be upset about this, but her reaction surprised me.

"Ugh, seriously? Again?" she practically grumbled. "I left. Why can't he just leave me alone? God, I hate that man."

She was upset, all right, but more angry than sad. Still, I'd take an angry woman over one who was crying any day. She remained silent for the rest of the ride, and I gave her space to sit with her thoughts. I needed to think too—about our options and how Archer, Vince, and I should handle this.

We pulled into the parking lot behind our building. I shut off the engine and turned toward her to get her full attention.

"I am very confident our building is secure, but he knows where you work now, and we live above it," I started to say. "I already touched base with Vince and Archer about adding some more cameras to the property, but until they can add those, I'm going to camp out on your couch."

"Wade, you're not sleeping on my couch," she started to say, but I cut her off.

"I would do the same for my sister or anyone of my friends' sisters too," I tried to justify so she didn't think I was trying to stay over for nefarious reasons. "More importantly, if I was overseas and either of my sisters had a stalker, I would want one of my friends to watch over my sisters too. Jack isn't here to stay with you, so I will."

"Wade, I wasn't fighting you on staying in the apartment," she said calmly. "As much as I hate to admit it, because I want to be a stronger person, I am a little freaked out how he was able to find me, especially since I didn't know the pub, security company, and the apartment were all in one building before I came here."

"Okay then, it's settled. I'll walk up with you first, but I'll go over and get a few things from my apartment in a little bit," I said as I turned to open my car door and exit, but she put her hand on my arm to stop me, and I felt a shock run up my entire arm. In a good way. Too good.

"Wade, I wasn't fighting you on staying in the apartment," she explained quickly and with a smile. "But I barely fit on that couch, and you are bigger than I am. You take the bed, and I'll sleep on the couch."

She pulled her hand off my arm, and I instantly wanted her to put it right back. While she made a good point, there was no chance I *wasn't* staying with her, so I figured my best course of action was to just get her back up to the apartment and get the details squared away later.

"We'll figure it out, but you're not staying alone tonight," I told her. "Let's head inside before it gets too hot sitting in this car."

We made our way upstairs, and I kept my eye on our surroundings the entire time. We went into her apartment to drop off the leftovers. She wanted to take a shower, so I left to go to my place to grab a few things and shower myself. I also needed to send some more detailed messages to Vince and Archer and get a game plan together for how to deal with this jackass if he showed up, because I had a feeling now that he knew she was here, it was only a matter of time before he made his presence known.

11

WADE

It was after six o'clock before I finally made it back over to Ellie's place. She opened the door with slightly wet hair and wearing an Army T-shirt and loose cotton shorts.

God, she looked good. I was pretty sure the shirt was her brothers, but I still felt a pang of jealousy that it wasn't my shirt she was wearing, putting my scent on her.

"You want to come in or just stand there?" she asked, smirking.

Crap. She clearly knew I was staring at her. I walked in and set my overnight bag on the floor by the door.

"I was just re-heating the food and was planning to watch a movie," she said, walking back toward the small kitchen. "Is that okay with you? If not, I can just watch a movie in the bedroom if you want to stay out here and do something else."

"Dinner and a movie sounds good," I told her. Though as soon as I said it, I regretted it. Not because I didn't want to eat, but because spending time with her in close prox-imity would test my will power.

I walked over to the couch, the one we would be sharing while watching a movie and the one I would be sleeping on tonight. The same one I helped Jack put together from IKEA. That was the biggest pain in the ass. I felt like all those LEGOs I played with during my child-hood should have better prepared me for building IKEA furniture, but alas, this L-shaped couch took two grown men almost two hours to put together.

I figured if I angled myself just the right way, I could probably get most of my body on this to sleep tonight. I grabbed two TV trays that Jack had in the corner and set them up in front of the couch, separating them as much as I could so we didn't have to sit right next to each other.

"I don't have much to offer to drink, but I have water, iced tea, and Dr. Pepper," she said as she turned and said from the kitchen.

"Water is fine, thanks," I told her, not needing the caffeine to keep me awake tonight since I would likely be restless enough on that couch.

I got up and walked to the kitchen, so she didn't have to carry everything in herself. We brought the food back and tried to figure out what movie to watch before settling on an action movie from a few years ago.

We'd chosen one of the Bourne movies, though I couldn't remember which one because I was trying to focus on my food and not her. I was on the chaise part of the couch, and she was in the opposite corner with her legs tucked up on her side. Her toes were only inches from me, and I was very focused on not letting them get closer.

After the movie, we carried the dishes into the kitchen. While she put everything away, I chose to use the restroom to get ready for bed. Normally I slept in just boxers, or at least shirtless, but I knew that likely wasn't my best option here, so I kept my gym shorts and T-shirt on.

After brushing my teeth, I came out to the living room to see her bent over, moving things around in the refrigerator. Her perfect ass was nicely on display. I stared at it for a moment, wondering what it would feel like in my hands. She stood back up and turned to me just as I moved my eyes to her face. She stared at me for a moment. I hoped my face didn't give away that I had just been looking at her ass.

"Ellie, I'm not sleeping in your bed," I insisted. She started to protest, but I cut her off. "I doubt anything will happen, but hypothetically, if someone were to break in through the front door, the couch is closer. I'm not putting you there. I'm on the couch. You sleep in the bed."

"Okay," she sighed. "I'm going to go change too and then I'll grab some blankets and a pillow for you."

As she walked back to her room, I grabbed a glass of water from the kitchen and my laptop so I could try to get a few things done for Archer so we could go ahead and hire Diego Martin.

A few minutes later, Ellie came out in a little pink

nightgown with a pillow and blanket. That nightgown was not a sexy material. In fact, it looked like it was very old cotton and was a bit loose on her, but there was no hiding her nipples peeking through the fabric. And just like that, my dick is hard, like I am a teenage boy who'd never seen a girl's boobs before.

Don't embarrass yourself, look away. Look. Away.

"Are you sure you want to sleep out here?" she asked quietly.

Was she asking me to stay in her room with her? Jack's bed was a queen. There was no way I could share that space with her and not touch her.

"I feel like I would fit so much better on the couch," she said, breaking me out of my thoughts. "I can take the couch, and you can sleep in the bed."

I realized my thoughts of sharing the bed were not what she was suggesting, but clearly my brain had gone there, and now my dick was getting hard just thinking about that unrealistic option. You'd never know I took care of myself in the shower earlier.

This was going to be a long night.

12

ELLIE

At some point in the middle of the night, I rolled over and looked at my phone to see it was just after midnight. I wasn't sure why I'd woken up, but I figured I might as well get up to pee since my body would likely wake me up soon to do it anyway.

As I was exiting the bed, I heard a noise. At first, I wasn't quite sure what it was. It sounded like a strangled groan, and then it got louder. I opened the bedroom door slowly and heard the noise again, louder this time, and realized it was coming from my living room. Knowing Wade was out there, I went over to make sure he was okay.

When I got closer, I realized he was still sleeping, but obviously having a dream – or from the sound of it, probably a nightmare. He started to jostle around quite a bit on the couch and started moaning louder. Then he started to whimper like he was in pain. I felt terrible and wanted to wake him but wasn't sure what to do.

My brother had nightmares sometimes when he was home on leave and he stayed with Gran and me, but I wasn't sure how Wade would react if I woke him. Just then, he swung his arm up high like he was swatting at something, and I realized if I didn't wake him, he would fall off the couch that he was already perilously half off of now. I decided to approach slowly and call to him quietly to try to wake him.

He didn't react the first time, so I moved closer. Crouching down next to the couch, put my hand on his shoulder and tried to shake him slightly to wake him.

It all happened so fast. One minute I was beside him, and the next he rolled off the couch in a swift calculated move and had me pinned to the ground with my hands above my head. He was straddled on top of me at the waist and breathing heavily as he pushed down on my hands to pin me in place.

"Ellie?" he gasped as he breathed heavily like he'd just run a marathon. "Shit! What are you doing? Are you okay? Did I hurt you?" he asked as he quickly moved off me and helped me up.

"Where does it hurt? Did I punch you? Where did I hit you?" He asked the rapid-fire questions as he looked over my arms and face, sliding his hands gently over my skin as though he was looking for injuries.

I grabbed his wrists quickly and stopped him.

"Wade, stop. You didn't hurt me," I rushed to reassure him. "I'm okay. I was just startled."

He let me go and sat back on the couch with his elbows on his knees and hands on his forehead, cupping the sides of his head. He was still breathing a little heavy as he scrubbed his hands over his face.

"Sorry. You were having a nightmare, and I was trying to wake you," I explained quietly since he seemed very upset. "I didn't mean to startle you. Are you okay?"

"Am I okay?" he asked, clearly perplexed, as his brows furrowed. "I just pinned you to the ground with all my weight because I thought you were attacking me, and you're asking if *I'm* okay? Christ, I just threw you around and could have injured you. Your ribs likely aren't fully recovered yet, and I almost broke you all over again. God, I'm so sorry."

I understood why he felt bad about pinning me down, and even that he was concerned about my ribs, but what confused me was his automatic assumption that he would injure me on purpose.

"Wade," I said, but his face was now buried back in his hands, and he didn't look up. I called his name again as I reached for his wrists to remove his hands so I could see his face.

"Why did you automatically assume that you hurt me?" I asked.

He looked at me, but the mask on his face hid any kind of emotion.

"Wade, your apology wasn't for accidentally falling on

me," I cautiously pressed. "You apologized as though it was a foregone conclusion that you injured me. Do you think I would assume that because of Randall?"

He stared at me for a few beats before sighing deeply and running his right hand through his hair. Then he looked back at me and started to explain about a woman named Candace, the nightmares, and the injuries he'd caused her.

Conversations I'd had with Tammy as well as comments his sister had made earlier today at his parents' house started to come back to me.

"So, you and my brother huh?" Wade's sister Whitney asked me, winking with a smile on her face.

"Oh no, we work together at the pub, and he served with my brother Jack, who's going into the security business with him," I told her with a smile.

"But he brought you to our family lunch, so it's clearly more," Willa said, and I could tell she was fishing. She was way off though, so I tried to explain to her.

"I'm not looking for a relationship right now, and Wade only sees me as his best friend's little sister," I told her.

She looked at me for a minute as the smile on her face grew impossibly bigger.

"Honey, any time you are within seeing distance, he can't take his eyes off you, and just saying, but he hasn't brought a girl home ever," she started to say and then looked toward Whitney. "He's too afraid to do a relationship after that bitch Candace."

There was so much to unpack in that comment that I

wanted to know more about but didn't have a right to ask. Instead, I just tried to wave off the significance of him bringing me, since I knew the only reason he'd brought me was because of what happened at the pub yesterday, but I didn't want to have to explain that to his sister.

"God, Ellie I'm sorry." Wade's words startled me back into the here and now. "Next time just let me have my nightmare but don't come near me to wake me, okay," he said, and I realized I hadn't reacted to anything he said while I went back to the conversation with his sister the day before.

He'd probably mistaken my silence for being upset with him or even agreeing with him.

"Is this why you don't date anyone?" I asked. He stared at me in confusion for a brief second before I explained. "Your sisters told me as much."

He huffed and rolled his eyes but brought them right back to me with such seriousness.

"My sisters meddle where they shouldn't, but yes, Candace made me realize that I can't do attachments, not until I get the nightmares under control," he said.

"Are you seeing someone about that?" I pressed, knowing that some people who had served didn't want to admit they had PTSD or see a therapist because they didn't believe it would help.

"Yeah," he said. "I'd like to be able to help my sister out with her kids sometimes, but I'm too afraid to fall asleep and have a nightmare around them right now."

As soon as he said it, he looked away, as though he

didn't really want me to know that part but it just kind of slipped out. I look at him and realized he was such a good man but was so afraid that his nightmares made him into a monster.

"Your ribs likely aren't fully recovered yet and I almost broke you all over again. God, I'm so sorry." That's what he'd said to me just a few minutes ago.

It occurred to me he was comparing pinning me down on the ground just now to what Randall did to me over a month before. He looked so distraught over it, I knew I needed to set him straight and make him realize the two were not the same.

"Wade, look at me," I said as sternly as I could to make sure I had his attention. "What Randall did to me was on purpose. He did that with the sole intention of hurting me. What you did to your ex, and what happened just now, was an accident and out of your control."

"It doesn't matter," he interrupted. "I still could have hurt you, and I *did* hurt her. I'm a soldier, Ellie. Even when I'm asleep, my body is trained for combat, so when I fight, that response is fight to kill."

I heard what he was saying, but I needed him to understand that there was a difference.

"I get that, but I also disagree," I emphasized. "The intention of the act absolutely does matter."

He looked away from me like he disagreed, but also didn't want to keep discussing this.

Looking at him, I realized he was everything I had ever hoped for in a boyfriend. Sexy, kind, protective, and smart. The kind of man I had always imagined. But he was never going to open himself up again—too afraid of hurting someone else.

He saw himself as damaged goods. I understood that. I felt that while I was with Randall and even after I left him.

Thanks to Katie, and even Tammy and Wade eventually, I found that other people saw me differently. They saw the good in me, even when I couldn't see it myself. I wanted to be that for Wade. I wanted to make him realize what a good person he was, despite his PTSD. I also wanted to show him that I wasn't scared of him and that I wasn't scared to be with him. I knew I had to be the one to initiate it, though, because he never would.

I lifted myself from sitting on the floor to up on my knees and crept closer to him, where he was sitting on the couch with his elbows still on his knees. His hands were on either side of his face as he looked down, and his legs were spread shoulder-width apart. He looked up at me and tracked me as I got closer. I moved to position myself between his legs, my face just a few inches from his. I looked at his mouth briefly and licked my lips, remembering what he tasted like, and then looked up at his eyes to see heat in them, but also concern.

"Ellie," he said in a low growl as he lifted his elbows off his knees and put his arms on the edge of the couch.

It was definitely a warning, but the way he growled my name like that, I felt that deep in my core. I knew what I wanted, and in that moment, I was going to make it happen. In part because I was selfish, and also because I wanted him to see that I knew he wasn't a monster and I wasn't afraid of him.

I put my hands on his knees and moved my face to within an inch of his, staring into his eyes.

My heart raced, and I felt my breath pick up as I focused on him—really seeing him. He wasn't perfect, but neither was I, not by a long shot. Looking into his gorgeous milk chocolate eyes, I saw something beyond the hesitations, the uncertainties. Beneath it all, he was a good man. A man who cared deeply about his friends and family, was a hard worker, a protector, and carried the potential for something great.

I took a breath, my mind made up. I was taking the next step, and if he wasn't quite there yet, that was okay. I was ready for the both of us. And maybe, just maybe, we could help each other heal.

I leaned forward slowly to at least give him a little warning and put my mouth to his. At first it was me kissing him, and after a few seconds of him sitting there frozen, I started to second-guess my decision. In the next instant, his hands were on either side of my face, thumbs along my cheeks and other fingers in my hair, and he was pulling my face, angling it to the side, and then he took over the kiss. He took full control. His tongue was now in the mix, and he tasted fantastic. I could get drunk off his taste.

I started to move my hands from the top of his knees back down his thighs so I could get closer to him. Wade had other plans because suddenly his hands were under my arms, and I was lifted off the ground and onto his lap. My nightgown rode up, so the bottom hem was bunched up at my sides and all that separated me from Wade was my thin layer of underwear.

He sat back onto the couch, looking up at me for a moment as if he were trying to soak me in and save it in his memory while simultaneously fighting with himself about what to do next. I licked my lips, tasting him on me.

"Screw it," he mumbled and then pulled my face down to his and started kissing me again. My stomach fluttered as I became dizzy from his kiss. God, what this man did to me. I felt spasms between my legs, and my body moved of its own volition as I rolled my hips forward and felt his length beneath me. It rubbed against all the right places, and I heard a moan come from my mouth at the same time his kiss became more intense. My brain started to short-circuit as his mouth roamed from my lips down to my neck and collarbone. His beard roughly moving across my neck both tickled and felt amazing. His hands moved to my hips and pulled me closer to him, pressing me down into his hips.

"Wade," I moaned as he thrust his hips upward hitting me in just the right spot, and I could feel my orgasm building.

His hands moved up my sides, and before I knew it, my nightie was gone. His mouth was on my nipple a moment later. My panties were soaked, and I was pretty sure my wetness was now making a spot on his shorts.

"God, Ellie, you are gorgeous," he growled with his lips just inches away from my breasts. He stopped moving, appearing to take in my whole body with his eyes, but I was close to orgasm. I could feel it, and I didn't want him to stop. I rolled my hips and mumbled his name.

"Wade, please." The groan was barely above a whisper, but his eyes moved to mine at my words.

"Be sure, Ellie," he said, his tone serious but also strained, like he was holding back. "We cross this line, we can't go back."

"I'm sure," I told him, looking right back into his eyes so he understood my sincerity." I want this, I want you."

He grabbed me behind my thighs and lifted me so he could put me on the couch, sitting upright with my legs spread open and hanging off the edge of the couch. With Wade on his knees in front of me, his dick, while still inside his clothes, was perfectly lined up at my entrance. He leaned in and kissed me, his hands going to my neck. I moved my hands too, wanting to feel his chest. Then he pulled back and stared at me.

The desire was clear in his eyes, but he was also looking at me reverently, which made me feel bare and exposed, and not just in the literal sense.

He leaned in and put his mouth on my nipple, sucking hard. I let out a high-pitched noise that had never come from my mouth before. His hand started moving south and began swirling near my entrance, which sent tingles through my whole body.

"God, Ellie, you're so wet," Wade murmured, his hot breath on my chest.

His finger slid inside, and I felt my orgasm building again.

"So damn wet and tight," he said as he slid another finger inside and used his thumb to rub my clit. "Your pussy is squeezing my fingers so tight. I can't wait to be inside you."

His words set me off, and my orgasm ripped through me so fast, the only sound I could make was a gasp with Wade's name barely coming out.

"God, you are beautiful when you come," he said, but my eyes were closed and I couldn't move.

I needed to focus on making sure I could get enough air back in my lungs. As I finally opened them, I saw him taking his shorts all the way off, reaching back, and grabbing a condom out from his wallet. He started to sheath himself and then looked straight at me.

"Be sure, Ellie," he said in a low voice. "Once is not going to be enough with you, so I need you to be really sure."

I still wasn't sure I could speak, as I was still breathing heavy, so I reached down for his shaft and barely got my fingers to graze it when he grabbed my wrist.

"Ellie, don't," he said as he used a hand to block mine. "You touch me, and I won't last. I'm barely hanging by a thread here."

"I want you inside me," I said softly, my eyes directly on his.

In the next moment, he grabbed my legs and pulled me so that my butt was on the edge of the couch, and then he drove inside me. Hard. His cock filled me to the brim, and I felt full and stretched and amazing all at once. He immediately started moving in and out as he brought his mouth to mine and kissed me hard. Every synapsis in my body was firing, and I felt him move even deeper inside.

My fingers dove into his hair, and gripped tightly as I enjoyed all the feelings coursing through my body. My heart hammered beneath my chest. Dear Lord this man felt amazing.

"Wade," I said, hoping he could hear the pleading in my voice.

Reaching back, I grabbed the cushion at the top of the couch to get leverage as he pumped in and out of me.

He removed his lips from mine as he drove deeper into me. "Let go, Ellie."

He moved his thumb to the bundle of nerves just above his dick, and I detonated.

Instantly, I felt warmth race through my body as my orgasm hit. I yelled out his name and then nothing. I think I may have blacked out. I vaguely heard him grunt my name, and then he slowed his movements.

With his face nestled in the crook of my neck, I could feel his hot breath on me, and I found I enjoyed that feeling.

"Damn, Ellie," he said, as his rapid breathing began to subside. "I'll be right back. Don't move."

That wouldn't be a problem. I was pretty sure none of my limbs were functioning anyway.

As I slowly came back to the real world, Wade walked into the room, completely unabashed by the fact that he was naked. He had a washcloth in his hands, and he knelt down in front of me and started to wipe the area between my legs with the warm, wet cloth.

"Are you okay," Wade asked, concern written on his face. "I didn't mean for that to be so fast. I'm sorry."

"I enjoyed it," I told him, and I had.

I liked that I'd made him lose control. That he was so into me, so caught up in the moment, that he lost focus of everything else.

He leaned forward into the crux of my legs and kissed me on my lips. It was light and soft at first, but then he slid his tongue in, and it started to get intense. He broke away and put his forehead to mine.

"Jesus, one kiss, and I'm ready to have you all over again," he said in a whisper, as though he didn't mean for me to actually hear his thoughts.

I looked down, and sure enough he was hard again. I didn't even know a guy could be ready that fast again. Didn't guys need like an hour recovery time or something?

"Maybe we should try a bed this time," I teased him. "There's one just down the hallway."

I smiled up at him, and something flashed in his eyes. Then he closed them. He looked briefly in pain.

"Babe, I can't be naked with you in a bed right now

and not have sex with you again," he said to me, almost distressed. "And I can't do that in Jack's bed. There's something sacrilegious about that, and I already feel guilty enough."

"Oh," I said in a low voice, frowning. That made me a little sad because I was starting to get excited about the idea of doing that again. "What about your bed?"

I realized as soon as I said it what I was implying. He'd just finished telling me women in his bed scared him because he was afraid of falling asleep. And he'd just had a nightmare already tonight. I shouldn't have suggested that. He clearly wasn't ready.

"I'm sorry. I..." I started to tell him, but he cut me off.

"Let's go," he said excitedly.

He picked me up then picked my nightgown up off the floor and handed it to me before setting me on my feet. Then he grabbed his clothes and threw his pants on but was carrying his shirt. As soon as I got dressed, he grabbed my hand and pulled me to the door, handing me my phone and keys as we walked out.

My mind was racing. Not only because of what we were about to do –again– but also the hurried nature of it had me feeling like I was forgetting something. My hands were shaking so bad as I tried to lock my apartment door. Wade suddenly came up behind me, took the keys, and did it for me. Once it was locked, I turned around to go to his place, but he hadn't moved, and the front of his body was only inches from the front of mine. He took a small step forward and pushed me up against my door.

"Calm down, Ellie. Take a breath," Wade said to me softly against my lips as he kissed me, slipping his tongue inside.

"I can't calm down if you're going to kiss me senseless," I told him when he pulled back. I couldn't believe I'd said that out loud.

His smirk returned to his face, and he grabbed my hand and walked me to his door. It was already unlocked. I realized he'd likely done that while I was struggling to lock my own.

We walked into his apartment, and I looked around his dark space and realized it was a mirror image of my brother's apartment. I heard him lock the door and set his keys down. I turned to face him, and he came up to me, put his hands on my hips, and stared at me. I looked down at him, still shirtless, getting a close-up look at his tattoos. I'd seen hints of them before, but he had several more on his chest that I could see now were very intricate. Without thinking, I started to run my fingers over the ink. He had a tribal pattern that started on his chest and meandered onto his shoulders and the upper portion of his arms. In the middle of his chest was the Army logo with several small dog tags, each with a letter on them.

"What are these?" I whispered, pressing my fingers to the dog tags.

"Tags of the guys I lost overseas," he said very matter-of-factly.

My heart ached for him because there were several tags on his chest. I ached for those soldiers too, who would never get to go home. I leaned forward and placed my lips on the logo, kissing him softly. I felt his hands at my hips squeeze a little tighter. I leaned back and looked up at him. His chocolate eyes were sparkling, even in the low light.

"What are you thinking about?" I asked him.

He didn't answer me. He simply leaned forward and kissed me. It was hard, heated, intense. I felt that heat move through my body. His hands, which were at my hips, started moving lower. Down my back and to the backs of my thighs. The next thing I knew he was lifting me up and moving my legs to wrap around his hips. My arms automatically wrapped around his neck. Then we were moving. His lips never broke from mine until I was on my back on a soft mattress.

Despite having just had sex less than ten minutes ago, I could already feel a budding orgasm taking shape. Wade must have been feeling the same, because the fire in his eyes and the urgency of his hands and mouth on my body showed he needed this as much as I did. However, unlike before, he took his time. He lingered, unhurried, and deliberate. As though he was discovering the nuances of my body that he had skimmed over the first go round.

Later, I lay there, completely sated, half asleep, and wrapped up in Wade's arms. I thought back to how crazy the last twenty-four hours had been, but knowing this was how it would end, I wouldn't change a thing.

13

WADE

I slowly woke to the smell of citrus fruits. I opened my eyes and realized that smell belonged to the blonde hair in front of me. The hair that was attached to the naked body I was currently spooning. Ellie's delicious body was up against mine, and my dick immediately took notice and hardened. After having sex in her apartment, we moved to mine because I could not bring myself to have sex with her in her brother's bed. Having sex with Jack's sister was already going to get me in hot water, but if I did it in his bed, he just might kill me.

After we moved to my place, I took her again, this time in my bed because I was a selfish bastard and needed to be close to her for reasons I really didn't want to think deeply about. Not once did I think about what would happen if I fell asleep and had a night terror. I chose to blame it on my brain not firing on all cylinders after two of the best damn orgasms of my life.

Waking up to her scent and delicious body up against mine made me never want to leave this bed. Remembering how soft her skin was every time I touched her last night made my dick impossibly harder. Last night was the best sex I'd ever had, bar none. The little noises she made when I kissed her and moved my hands all over her body had me fighting not to be a two-pump chump. Even on the second go last night, I felt like a teenager who couldn't control his hormones and was ready to blow after being inside her for mere seconds.

Sex with other women was good too. I felt satisfied but ready to go home after finishing. With Ellie, I was ready to go all over again after just a few minutes of recovery. She had that effect on me. Her body was addictive.

Even now, just her body pressed up against mine while sleeping, and I was ready to go again. This woman's body was like voodoo to my dick. I snuggled up against her, my hands roaming over her warm, naked body, and kissed her neck and shoulders. God, this woman was a drug I couldn't get enough of.

Before I got serious in my pursuit of taking her again, my phone buzzed from the nightstand. I reluctantly separated from her and reached behind me to grab my phone. I saw a few texts from Archer telling me that he and Vince were on their way over. They found a few things and needed to talk to both Ellie and me. I'd told them yesterday I was going to stay on the couch in her apartment because of what happened, so they'd texted they were headed to her apartment.

I shot them back a thumbs-up reply, realizing I needed to get us both up and dressed and back in her apartment before they came over. The guys knew we'd stayed in the same apartment, but I wasn't ready for the conversation with them about the other stuff that took place in the apartment last night, or that we ended up moving to my apartment and my bed.

I turned back around, put my hand on her shoulder, and tried to wake her.

"Ellie, we gotta get up," I said in her ear, which only made it worse because I took in her scent again and my brain struggled. "Archer and Vince are on their way over."

She moaned and pushed her soft body right back up against me, and my dick protested that we were not going to remedy this situation. I had to get up and get away from her before I lost control and Vince and Archer heard me hooking up with her from the hallway.

"Ellie, the guys will be here in a few minutes. We need to get up and get dressed," I told her as I made my way from the bed to the dresser.

I heard her rouse and rustle under the covers, but I didn't want to see her naked body since I was trying to get my dick under control, so I grabbed my clothes and walked out into the kitchen area. I headed over to my coffeemaker, hoping to pump some caffeine into my body since I was exhausted from not having much sleep the past two nights.

"Wade," Ellie called my name from the hallway.

"Umm, I don't have any clothes other than my nightgown."

I looked down to see her in that damn pink nightgown that looked amazing on her, but I realized I didn't want Archer and Vince to see her like that. I tried not to dwell on the fact that having other men see her dressed like that made me jealous.

"Let's just go over to your place, then. We can make coffee there," I told her as I grabbed my favorite kind from the counter.

We walked across the hall, and she went to change while I got coffee going in her kitchen.

We weren't even in there for five minutes before there was a knock on the door. I opened it to allow Archer and Vince to walk inside. Archer started to tell me something in a low voice as Ellie rushed into the room with short jean shorts that showed off her amazing long legs and another Army T-shirt that still gave me a weird sense of jealousy. I turned to look at my friends before my dick started to harden and I embarrassed myself, only to see Vince's eyes on me, very calculated, like he was trying to read my thoughts.

"I'm sorry. I was going to try to make some breakfast before you guys got here," she rushed to say as she pulled her hair into a ponytail and darted into the kitchen area. "Just give me a few minutes, and I'll whip something up real quick," she said over her shoulder.

"It's really not necessary, Ellie. We already ate, but thanks," Archer told her politely.

I looked back over to Vince, who was looking back and forth between Ellie and me, and I started to get a little nervous that he knew exactly what happened and he could see through my smooth exterior.

"Are you sure?" she asked, clearly upset that she had not been a good host or something. "What about coffee? Wade started that, so it should be ready?"

They both agreed to that and started to move into the living room area, where they sat on the couch. I followed them in, and Archer started to talk low again to me, clearly wanting to tell me something that Ellie couldn't hear.

"Started looking into some things, and I need to take a look at her car," he started to say before Ellie came into the room and handed them both a coffee.

"So, what did you guys want to talk about?" Ellie looked at them with a bit of unease, even though she was trying to cover it with her shoulders back and a tight smile on her face.

Archer and Vince both looked at each other, and Vince leaned forward like he was going to ask her for something he wasn't sure she was going to agree to.

"Before we get to that, I was wondering if I could borrow your car for a few hours today since mine is in the shop," he asked her, and I knew something was up. Even if Archer hadn't just given me a heads-up, Vince's car was less than a year old, so there was no way there was something wrong with it that would need checked out. Not to mention very few mechanic shops were open on a

Sunday, but I wasn't going to call him out on that since I knew there was more to the story.

"Umm, sure. I work at the pub today, so I shouldn't need it," she told him. "Although, my car is small. Wade's SUV is bigger if you need it for something to haul."

Vince paused a second, clearly not expecting that response, though he was quick on his feet and recovered smoothly.

"I, uh, remembered Wade mentioning he had some kind of appointment thing today, and I knew you were working, so I figured it would just be easier, but if it's an inconvenience, I can..." he started to say, playing into her need for hospitality, before she cut him off.

"Oh no, it's totally fine. Please take it!" she all but insisted as she waved her hands up. "I'll go get the keys!"

She darted back over to the kitchen to get the keys from her purse.

Vince looked over at me quickly and mumbled to just play along. I nodded knowing he would fill me in when he could.

"It doesn't have much gas in it. I'm sorry," Ellie said as she handed him the keys.

"All good, Ellie. I'll get some gas while I'm out," he told her.

"No, please don't. I can get some after you return it, although if it runs out and you have to, I can pay you back," she insisted.

He started to argue with her, but she cut him off.

"Stop!" she sighed before taking in a shaky breath.

"You guys don't understand. You gave my brother a friendship when he needed it the most, and he always talked about you and how you had his back—well except for you, Archer, since you didn't serve with him." She grinned and looked at Archer. "But you guys are his brothers in all the ways that matter, and now you are my brothers too, so let me do this for you," she said to us, and while I felt my heart pinch at the kind words she'd said, it also made me feel a little irritated because she thought of me as a brother, and we'd just had sex last night.

"All good, Ellie," Vince told her, and she smiled.

"Okay," she said, and clapped her hands together. "Was that what you guys came here to talk about, or was there something else?"

"One more thing. What's Randall's last name?" Archer asked.

"Rupnik. His full name is Randall Richard Rupnik Junior," she answered.

Archer nodded, and I knew he would be reaching out to some friends he still had on the force.

"We also came to talk with Wade about the business, but I'll also tell you to be careful coming and going from the pub," Archer cautioned. "Your ex has obviously figured out you work there, so we want to be vigilant. When Wade is working, he's going to escort you in and out of the building, but when he's not, we'll make sure someone is with you. Got it?"

She nodded and agreed to his terms, though I could see she wasn't happy about it.

"I'm gonna borrow Wade while Vince takes your car, but I promise one of us will be back to walk you to work before your shift, okay?" Archer told her, and she nodded.

"We'll be across the hall in his apartment if you need anything," he said as he got up to leave.

"I know you guys are trying to protect me, and that's great, but I'll be fine here by myself. I'm just going to do some laundry and cleaning," she said, clearly trying to act braver than she likely was feeling on the inside.

"You said it yourself. We're your brothers now too, so give us the one perk of being a brother and let us be over-protective," Vince said while smirking at her.

"Touché," she laughed. "I'll lock up after you leave."

I walked out the door with both of them, but they waited until we got inside my apartment before talking.

Vince decided he was going to be first.

"Where did you sleep last night?" he asked me, but I could tell there was accusation in his tone.

"I slept here in my bed," I told him, which was the truth. I just left out a few details.

"You left her at her place alone?" he asked, a little shock in his voice. "I thought you were sleeping at her place on her couch?"

"She insisted Jack's couch was too small for me to fit on, and she would rather take the couch here so I could sleep in my own bed." Also not a lie, but also not the whole truth. But I wasn't ready to have this conversation with him about what Ellie and I were since I wasn't even sure myself. That was also a lie, since I knew she had worked her way under my skin and wasn't likely to get out.

"Then why were you back at her place this morning?" he accused me again, and I could tell he knew I was withholding from him.

"You told me you were meeting at her place, so we walked back over," I answered him.

"Guys, enough," Archer intervened clearly not interested in whatever interrogation Vince was set on giving me.

Taking advantage of his break, I decide to start asking questions.

"Why are you taking her car when I know full well your car has nothing wrong with it and you also know I don't need mine today," I asked Vince, but my eyes were focused on Archer since I wasn't ready to look Vince in the face yet.

"Go take a look at her car and I'll explain the rest to him," Archer said to Vince who nodded and walked out the door.

I looked over to Archer, waiting for news I had a feeling I wasn't going to like.

"You said she told you she doesn't think the ex knew where in Georgia she was headed, and I believe her. Jack confirmed he first told Ellie his address right before she moved here," Archer started to explain, but I honed in on one point.

"You talked to Jack about this?" I asked wondering how he took that.

"Yeah," he confirmed. "I know we all talked about it, but right after the phone call at the bar, I started having some questions myself. Vince reached out to some contacts you guys still have over there to get in touch with him ASAP. He's pissed and ready to kill that mother fucker, but also couldn't talk long since he's knee deep in his mission. He answered a few questions we had and said as soon as this mission is done, he's signing his exit paperwork and taking the first flight home."

He paused, as if carefully choosing his words next. "You said she mentioned that she originally left him without taking her stuff, and she waited until her friend could go with her to retrieve them a few days later, at a time she *knew* he was supposed to be working," he said as I nodded to confirm. "So, it's not just that he knew she was here at the pub, but he also knew when she arrived at his house to collect her things, very quickly I might add."

"You know how he found her." It was a statement because it was the only reason why he would bring this up.

He nodded, then continued. "My working theory is that he put a tracker on her car. If he knew where she worked, he could have gone there one day during her shift and put it on her car, knowing she would have to come back at some point to collect her things, and he would want to know when that was."

"Shit," I growled, knowing this was entirely plausible but also not liking where he was going with this.

"He showed up at the house moments after she did,

beat her, and left—probably assuming she would still be there when he returned a few hours later. She wasn't. But he realized she had only moved the car a few blocks away —something we know she did temporarily while staying with her friend because she didn't want him to have access to her car."

All the dots were connecting in my head from Ellie's story, and it made sense, but also made me livid. Thinking about how he stalked her, only to beat her senseless, had me raging.

He sensed my anger and told me to calm down and let him finish.

"A few days later, when she was recovered enough to make the long drive, she retrieved her car and moved here. He connects the dots once he pings her location to realize she's parked behind a building that has both a restaurant as well as a security company."

"Ellie said she told him her brother was, quote 'starting up a new business with his Army buddies,' but didn't give him any details about it or the fact that it was a security business," I told him, seeing where his mind was going.

"Okay, well, even if he didn't know about Ranger Shield, she used to work at a pub, and there is a pub right next to where her car has been parked pretty much night and day for the last few weeks. My guess is he kept calling there, hoping to hear her voice or confirm she works there, and he did. Which is why he called again when Tammy worked because he wanted to torment her again."

"So, Vince is checking her car for a tracking device?" I asked, assuming that was why he needed to "borrow" her car.

"Yeah," he confirmed. "We didn't want to worry her if I was wrong."

I understood that, but my guess was he wasn't wrong.

"What do we do when you are correct?" I asked him, letting him know I thought his suspicions were more than valid.

He smiled, clearly appreciating my confidence in how his mind worked, but then his smile changed.

"Hold that thought. Before Vince gets back, I wanna talk about something else," he said, his eyes boring into mine. "I checked the cameras in the building this morning to make sure we didn't have any blind spots in any of the entrances or exits."

I nodded, not sure where he was going with this.

"Also wanted to check the hallway on this level so I could see in case someone did actually gain access, I wanted to be able to see them clearly from the moment they got off the elevator and all the way to your door and Jack's," he said.

I now realized where he was going with this. He'd seen Ellie and me leave her apartment last night and head to mine. He'd seen me kiss her up against the door. I cursed every possible word I knew in my head. How could I have forgotten the cameras?

"I don't know Jack as well as you and Vince since I didn't serve with him, but I'm still happy to take on the brotherly role of protector for her," he said, staring right at me. "Do I need to be stepping in as a brother right now?"

His question wasn't asked in anger, but rather as a message. A message of "it's none of my business, but at the same time it is." I didn't know how to answer him because I honestly didn't know what Ellie and I were myself, but I also needed him to know that.

"I won't do anything to hurt her," I told him, which I knew was vague, but I also didn't really want to get into it with him.

"I didn't say you would," he started to say, but was interrupted.

Just then the door opened and Vince walked in, holding something.

"Found it." He held out his phone, showing a photo he took of a little transmitter device. "Asshole didn't even hide it that well, so I'm guessing he thought he'd have her back and would be able to remove it himself before anyone figured it out."

"Now what do we do?" I asked, feeling myself get angry again.

"Now, we mess with him," Vince said.

I looked over at the two of them and watched them exchange a look, realizing they must have already come up with a plan.

"Remember, Tammy said she told Randall over the phone yesterday that Ellie doesn't work there anymore—so we play off that," Vince noted.

"We move her car to my apartment complex for now,

which is the most secure of anyone's, and I've got plenty of cameras around and gated access," Archer explained. "We also take turns driving it to a couple other pubs around town to make him think she's looking for a new job. This will buy us some time to do more digging into this asshole."

"Are we going to tell her what's going on and why she can't have her car back?" I asked, knowing she would be fine with one day but would start to get suspicious if he kept asking every day to borrow her car.

"We can, and honestly, it may be good for her to realize how seriously whacked-out this guy is and would allow us to keep a closer eye on her," Archer said. "Or we can also tell her that Vince got into a little fender bender today and will get her car fixed but will take a few more days."

Both options were good, but I figured Ellie would be pissed if she knew we were hiding something from her, and, selfishly, it would give me an excuse to keep her close.

"I say we tell her. Otherwise, she'll be pissed if she finds out we withheld this information," I told them. "And you're right, hopefully it will make her be more vigilant."

"And also give you an excuse to keep her sleeping at your place," Vince said with a hint of accusation in his voice.

Shit. Archer brought it up specifically when Vince was

out of the room, so I didn't think he knew what had already transpired, but still.

"Also, if Rupnik's been paying attention," Archer added. "He'd have noticed she hasn't moved her car at all during the night the last few weeks. So, he either thinks she's sleeping at the pub or is living in the building."

"There's no way he can get up to these apartments without the code and a key. Plus, we have dozens of cameras everywhere," I interjected. "But if she feels more comfortable staying with one of us, then I don't see the problem with that."

The guys just nodded at my response, and I took that as a win for now. I sent her a text to tell her the guys and I wanted to chat with her, and she messaged back right away to come over. The guys and I discussed how we wanted to handle this then walked over there.

She opened the door with a smile, but when she saw all three of us standing there, instantly the smile dropped from her face.

"Something tells me you aren't here for good news," she said cautiously as she opened the door more and let us in.

We explained how the guys found the tracker on her car and how that was likely not only how he knew she was at the pub, but also how he knew she'd arrived at his house to pack up her things.

"This is why you wanted to borrow my car, wasn't it?" she asked with clear sadness in her voice as she took this all in.

We confirmed and explained how we thought we should proceed using her car to throw him off by moving it around.

"Do I need to move out of Jack's apartment if he knows I was here?" she asked nervously.

"You can always stay with me if you want. I have an extra room, and my building is also secure," Vince said, and I instantly glared at him. I stopped myself after a couple seconds, realizing I didn't want to give anything away, but he briefly smirked at me, which meant he did it on purpose to get under my skin, and I now knew he realized something else was going on. Shit.

"This building is incredibly secure, and the odds of him getting in here to this apartment are extremely small, but if you'd rather stay somewhere else, we can make that happen," Archer said, sensing the growing tension between Vince and me and trying to take over.

"Okay, um, I think I'd like to stay here if you think it's safe," she said, trying to sound a bit more confident.

"You should be fine, but I'm always across the hall if you need anything," I said to let her know I was here, but I also didn't offer to stay with her right in front of Vince and Archer.

"What will I do when I need to use my car though?" she asked.

"One of us can take you whenever you need to go somewhere. We have a special company vehicle that we can use," Archer told her, and I was glad he did, because I hadn't thought of that.

We had two vehicles we'd bought for the business to use as needed. One was an older model sedan that was nothing special but would blend in if we needed to do recon or get into places unnoticed. The other was an SUV that had all the bells and whistles and extra security features. This was the one he was likely referring to.

"Okay, thanks," she said. "I'm supposed to meet Ruthie tomorrow to go with her to her self-defense class."

This was a surprise to me, but I was glad she was going to that because it would be very helpful. I was also happy she was making friends. I didn't know much about Ruthie, but she seemed nice. She also didn't appear to have any local friends either since she moved here at the same time Archer did.

"I can take you both to that," Archer said before I had the chance to offer.

"Oh no, I can just borrow one of the cars. There's no need for you to drive out of your way to get us both," Ellie responded and I was about to offer myself, but Archer cut in.

"It's not out of my way, Ellie," Archer interrupted smoothly. "Ruthie lives in my same apartment complex, and we sometimes drive to work together any way. I can take you both and then drop you back off when we come into the office."

"Oh, okay. I didn't realize you both lived in the same complex," she said, and I realized I didn't know that either. I didn't know much about Archer, other than he was Vince's cousin, grew up in Vegas, used to be a cop until something bad happened, or maybe a few bad some-things happened, and one of his sticking points with starting the new company with us was that Ruthie was going to be our secretary. I also vaguely recalled Vince saying he may have also been married once, though I wasn't sure about that.

I put those thoughts on the back burner for now. Archer and Ellie finished up their conversation about the self-defense class, and then we all went our separate ways. I really did have a few errands to run, so Archer was going to drop Ellie off at work while Vince went and moved her car.

Since I didn't want to talk about it in front of the guys, I made plans to talk to Ellie about what happened last night after we were done at the pub tonight. Plus, this would give me time to get my own thoughts together on what I want to do, since at this point, I really didn't have one single clue.

14

ELLIE

I walked into the pub, happy to see Tammy there already, and I smiled and waved at her quickly as I went to put my purse in the break room before coming back to the bar to work with her. As I rounded the back and came into the bar area, she was staring at me with the biggest smile on her face, and I couldn't help it if hers was contagious and it made me smile too.

"Looks like somebody had fun last night," she said as she leaned in closer to me so that no one else could hear us. My smile instantly turned into a shocked face. How did she know that? Did Wade tell her? She laughed and leaned in again.

"Girl, if you don't want to talk about the details, that's fine, but it's written all over your face that you had a good night last night. I'm just happy one of us got lucky." She winked at me.

I could feel my face flush as embarrassment took over.

I stood there speechless for a few moments before her voice startled me back into the present.

"Here," she said, handing me a fresh draft beer. "While I swap the first keg, take this to Ted, and you can go ask Jimmy what he wants, though I can already tell you he wants an order of potato skins and Dr. Pepper," Tammy informed me.

"How the hell do you remember everyone's name and order all the time?" I asked her.

"Girl, my superpowers are remembering every one of my customers' names and leaving laundry in the dryer until it wrinkles. Then turning the dryer on to de-wrinkle, and then forgetting about them all over again," she said while laughing.

I laughed too because I'd definitely done that a few times.

"Well, mine are dating red flags and picking the slowest line at the grocery store every single time," I told her, and she burst out laughing.

"We'll circle back about that first one later, but let me get these kegs changed out first," she said before she walked into the back.

I knew she was going to ask more about it because that was how Tammy was, but she was also a great listener, and so far, appeared to give great advice, so maybe it wasn't a bad thing. Maybe I should also plan to pick her brain about Wade. I could really use a female friend to talk to about this. Normally I would call Katie, but she was on vacation with her cousins, and I wanted her to enjoy that time off since she rarely got it, what with going to school and working full time. I'd catch her up when she got back. In the meantime, maybe Tammy could offer some advice.

We hit a slow point in the evening, and Tammy and I were sitting back just drying some of the glasses and putting them where they needed to be. I thought I'd begin to get evening close prep done early. Tammy, however, had different plans for our free time.

"Okay girl, talk," she said grinning at me.

"Umm, talk about what?" I tried to deflect, but she looked at me like I was stupid and waited for me to respond.

"First let's talk about what had you grinning like a loon when you walked in here today, and then let's talk about these red flags you seem to date," she said with her full attitude on display.

I sighed and gave in, hoping maybe I could get some good advice out of her.

"Wade and I had sex last night, a few times actually, and now I don't know what to do or how I'm supposed to act around him because we work together and I'm going to see him all the time, and I don't want it to be weird or awkward, especially if he didn't really enjoy it, because he lives across from me, and I can't exactly escape him," I rambled quickly spilling all of that out at once.

"Take a deep breath, Ellie," She chuckled lightly. "First, I saw that boy today, and he had the same damn grin on his face that you did when you walked in, so I'm guessing he enjoyed it just fine. Second, that boy isn't dumb, so I doubt he would have taken that step with you knowing it would turn into several levels of awkwardness, especially knowin' who your brother is, if he was just lookin' for a quick lay."

I knew what she was saying made sense, but I didn't have a lot of experience with this sort of thing, and I told her that.

"Tammy, I've only slept with two other guys. The first was my boyfriend in high school who I dated for a year before I let him get that far. The second guy is the big red flag I mentioned, so I don't exactly have a long history of what to do in this situation, and half of that history was a very bad decision."

She was quiet for a few moments before speaking.

"Couple quick questions." She rolled right into it. "Was the first one a red flag too, or just the second one?"

"Umm, well, the first one broke up with me two days after I gave him my virginity, but other than being a jerk, I'm not sure that makes him a red flag."

"The red flag the one responsible for the bruises you were wearing when you first got here?" she asked with a bit of sympathy on her face.

Ugh. I couldn't believe I'd thought my makeup would cover that. Clearly, I'd done a terrible job. I nodded at her.

"He the one that called here the other day?" she asked.

Not really wanting to talk about it in detail, I just nodded to her. She accepted my desire to not talk about it and moved on, but I could see her jaw get tight like she was fighting getting angry on my behalf.

"Right, I'm no fortune teller, so I can't tell you whether or not you and Wade are gonna make it in the long run, but what I can say is that I've known that boy a while, and I know his family raised him well. I say this because if you were ever going to get back into the dating game after dating those two previous assholes, Wade seems like he would be a good choice. He knows you work here, and he knows you live upstairs. More importantly, he knows your brother will probably kill him if he hurts you, regardless of the friendship they have between them. Same probably goes for Vince and Archer. That's all to say that I don't think he would jump into this without thinking of those things."

I exhaled, not realizing I'd been holding my breath while she was talking.

"With that said..." She put her hand on my shoulder. "You do what you feel comfortable with, hon."

I gave a little nervous laugh because I knew she was being nice, but also, she was probably right.

The rest of the shift was relatively easy-going, but by the end of it, I was dead on my feet.

Finally done, I headed back to the break room to grab my phone and purse. I saw Wade in the office as I walked back and popped in to let him know I was just going to grab my bag and we could head upstairs. I'd been thinking about it all night, but now that we were about to head up, I was even more nervous. We hadn't had the conversation of sleeping arrangements for tonight, and I didn't know how to bring it up. With my purse in hand, I walked back toward the office and saw Wade standing in the doorway, locking it up for the night.

"Ready?" he asked.

I was still so full of nerves, I couldn't get any words out. Instead, I simply nodded and started walking to the main room of the pub so we could go out the front door.

He moved his hand to the small of my back and walked closely behind me. I knew he wasn't doing it on purpose, but his proximity was making me even more nervous. I felt his hand burning a hole through my clothes at my lower back. We walked past the bar, and Wade stopped us to talk with Tammy.

"Office is locked up for the night, but if you need to change anything to the schedule, just let yourself in," Wade told her, his hand still stuck to my back, and I knew Tammy saw it.

"You got it, boss-man," she said with a big grin on her face. "Alright, kids, you have a good night. Don't do anything I wouldn't do, or maybe you should." She gave us an exaggerated smirk then cackled a little.

I saw Wade shake his head at her with a small grin, and turn toward me. I could feel my face blushing at Tammy's comment and didn't want him to see, so I turned toward the door and started walking to it. I felt the loss of his hand immediately, but he quickly caught up and instead put his arm around my shoulder.

"Slow down, speed demon," he said to me, and we were about to go through the front door. "We'll get upstairs eventually. No need to rush."

Oh God. He thought I wanted to get upstairs to jump his bones again. This was so embarrassing. I knew I needed to clear the air so he didn't think I was some kind of slut ready to pounce. I stopped and turned toward him, looking up into his eyes.

"I, uh, wasn't rushing because I want to...um...get in your...um...pants or anything," I started to explain. "I was just hungry and tired, so I just wanted to get upstairs quickly, that's all." I said it in a rush, knowing most of it was an exaggeration to try to downplay the situation.

I knew my face was pink and was likely getting worse when I saw the growing grin on his face.

"I wasn't implying you were, Ellie," he said softly with the grin still on his face. "I just need you to stay by my side as we walk outside, but good to know where your mind is at." He winked at me then pushed the door open in front of me and nudged me out and toward the other end of the building, where the entrance to the security office and apartment elevators were.

It was a good thing I was now turned away from him and walking in front, because my face could not possibly be any redder than it likely was right now. Ugh. I couldn't believe I just word vomited all of that to him.

We walked in silence to the elevators, and Wade pushed the button for the third level.

"I want you staying with me tonight," Wade started to say. "Let's pack you a bag then head over to my apartment. I need to shower, but we can order some food and watch a movie, okay?"

That was a lot to take in at once, so I just nodded as we got off the elevator and headed to my apartment.

"Pack clothes for tonight and tomorrow so you don't have to walk back over to your apartment tomorrow in your nightgown." The way he said that made it seem like he was angry I'd walked across the hall. I wasn't sure why, though, because it wasn't like anyone was there to see me.

He followed me inside while I packed a few things, including my crochet supplies, since I wasn't sure what his plans were for us.

We walked back over to his apartment, and he took a bunch of delivery menus out of his kitchen drawer. His phone buzzed in his pocket, and he took it out while I glanced at the menus.

"I have to call Archer real quick about something," he said, then circled a few things on each menu. He told me to pick whatever I want and to just order him one of the items he'd circled, depending on which restaurant I picked. He then headed down the hall, and I just set my bag over on the couch for now since I wasn't sure where to put it.

I figure if he'd wanted bar food, we would have just gotten it from downstairs, so I opted for Chinese food instead. I placed our order and got out some plates and silverware from his kitchen to busy myself while I waited. He came out ten minutes later and asked what I'd chosen.

"I got us Chinese. It should be here in another ten minutes," I told him.

"Okay, cool. I'll go downstairs and get it," he said, but the look on my face must have shown my confusion. "They can't get up here without a key or access code."

As soon as he said it, I realized this wasn't just a normal apartment complex, where you could just buzz people up.

He sat on the couch and grabbed the remote, pulling up Netflix. I brought the plates and utensils in with me to set on the coffee table.

After looking through the movies, we picked one we both liked. He got it set up and then went downstairs to get the food. He was only gone for five minutes, but it felt so much longer, as my brain went through every possible scenario of what could happen tonight. Was I sleeping on the couch? The bedroom? Where was he sleeping? Were we going to have sex again? I certainly would like to, but I didn't know how Wade felt about it.

Wade came back a few moments later with the food, and we relaxed on the couch. His was much bigger than my brother's, and we could both spread out with plenty of room, though I wasn't purposely trying to avoid him. I just didn't know what to do or how to play this.

After dinner, I asked him if I could shower quickly before we finished the movie. I hadn't planned to, but now realized it would give me a chance to clear my head as well as clean the bar smell off.

I returned to the couch wearing a pair of shorts and a camisole. We settled in to finish the movie, and somewhere along the line, I must have dozed off, because I vaguely awakened to Wade carrying me to a bed. I heard noises behind me and saw the bathroom light go on, but I must have been too exhausted, because moments later I was back to sleep and dead to the world.

I woke to movement and noises. As my eyes fluttered open, I realized the noises and movements were coming from Wade, who was next to me in the bed. He was mumbling and his body was twitching, and I realized he was having another night terror.

I'd tried to read up on night terrors during my break today, and from what I'd read, it said it was best not to wake them. Just try to calmly get them back into a normal peaceful sleep. Waking them or having physical contact with them, such as restraining their arms or moving them, could often make it worse. I lay there whispering calming words and trying to coax him back to rest, while keeping an eye on his movements in case I needed to adjust my position.

As I watched him move and groan, I couldn't help but think of my brother and wonder if he had these nightmares as well. Logically I knew he probably did since

PTSD was common in soldiers, but it made me sad thinking about it. I hoped he was talking to someone about it. I made a mental note to ask Wade about that later.

At some point, his body relaxed. During the episode, his body had moved so that he was now on his side facing away from me. I took a chance and gently put my hand on his back, running it softly up and down. He didn't flinch or move, so I keep rubbing it and speaking softly to him. He rolled over onto his back as he slowly looked at me, his eyes half-mast.

"Why're you awake?" he asked softly, his voice groggy.

I debated whether or not to tell him the truth, but I knew he needed to know, and I wanted him to under-stand that he hadn't hurt me.

"You had another night terror," I explained gently.

His eyes opened fully, and he rolled over to face me as he lifted his hand to my face, then shoulder and arm, as though he was checking me over for marks.

"Did I hurt you?" he asked, his voice strained a bit.

"No," I told him. "The internet said I shouldn't wake you but just talk softly to you and let you fall back into a normal sleep, so that's what I did. I was just rubbing your back to test if the episode was done. I'm sorry if I woke you."

"The internet told you?" he asked, looking at me funny.

"Yeah." I stared at him. "I wanted to know what I

could do if it happened again. There's a lot of really good information about night terrors online."

"And I didn't touch you or hurt you?" he asked, like he was unsure if my process had worked. He seemed convinced that he must have done something bad.

"No," I said firmly. "You started moving around and making agitated noises, but I scooted back and just started talking softly to you, and eventually your body calmed and you settled back to sleep."

He stared at me silently, and I could see the wheels turning in his head. He'd seemed tense since I'd accidentally woken him, but now he seemed to relax a bit.

"Come here," he murmured, pulling me into his front, and rolling me so that we were in a spooning position.

I didn't quite know what to make of this, but I let it go for now. A few minutes later, I felt myself dozing back off again, when I heard him whisper into my hair.

"Thank you."

I didn't know if he actually meant for me to hear it or not, so I didn't say anything. I just let myself drift back off to sleep, but this time with a smile on my face.

I woke up alone the next morning. I could hear the shower going and realized Wade must have already gotten up. I decided to get up too since I was waiting tables today for the lunch shift. I was in the kitchen getting some coffee going when Wade walked in. He was wearing Army green cargo pants and a tight black tee. His hair was still slightly damp, and he looked so hot. I just stood there and stared at him for a few awkward moments until he spoke and broke my brain of its thought process.

"What's on tap for today?" he asked, looking at me.

"Umm," I said as I tried to get my brain to focus. "I'm working the lunch shift and then going with Ruthie to the self-defense class after she gets off work. I think we're going to do dinner afterward."

"Archer driving you to all that?"

"Definitely the first thing, but I'm not sure about dinner," I told him realizing I should text Ruthie and ask.

"If he can't, text me and I'll take you," he stated. "Want you covered until we can get some more details on your ex, okay?"

I nodded.

"I'm heading out," he said as he grabbed some stuff off his counter. "I gotta meet Vince for some help with a skip, but text Archer or me when you need to head down to work, and one of us will walk you."

I started to protest that I didn't need protection for that short of a walk since I literally was living above the pub, but before I could tell him, his phone rang and he picked it up.

"Yeah," he said quickly. "Now? Okay, I'm on my way down now."

"Text one of us on your way down. I mean it, Ellie," he emphasized as he grabbed his keys and took one of them off. "Use this to lock up. I'll see you tonight."

Then he was gone and out the door with me holding the key to his apartment. It all happened so fast, I wasn't sure what to make of it. So I tried to just push it aside for now and get on with my day. I would think about it later when I had more time. I locked up and went back over to my apartment and got in the shower, did some laundry, and got ready for work.

Knowing Wade was likely busy because he was helping Vince with a skip, I decided to just text Archer about having him walk me to the pub. Plus, I could ask him about the driving situation for the self-defense class and dinner afterward.

He walked me over and told me he would drive us both to everything and just to meet them in the front office to Ranger Shield at 4:30. He also made me promise to text him if no one was around to walk me back to the building after I finished work.

Tammy was working behind the bar, and we had a rather mundane day at work, which I was happy about since I'd had had enough crazy in my life recently. I didn't need work to make things more complicated.

Tammy also walked me back over to the apartment entrance after my shift since she said she needed to chat with Archer about something anyway. I went upstairs to get changed for the class. I'd never done a self-defense class before, but I imagined you moved around a lot. Thus, you would need to wear clothing that would allow you the freedom to move. I figured my tight spandex shorts and a semi-loose tank top over a sports bra would be best. Though I packed some jeans and a T-shirt for dinner afterward.

I walked into the front office, expecting to see Ruthie, but instead I saw Archer and Wade talking to each other in low tones. Both of them looked up as I walked in. I noticed Wade was eyeing my choice of workout clothes with an intensity that seemed to be a toss between approval and anger.

"Hey, Ellie," Archer said to me, and then he mumbled something to Wade as he started walking from the desk over to me.

"Um, hi," I said awkwardly moving my gaze from Wade over to Archer. "Where's Ruthie?"

"She's already in my car out front. We're ready when you are," he said as he moved past me and out the door. I started to follow but felt Wade come up behind me.

"Have fun," he said as he squeezed my shoulders. He didn't kiss me or show any other signs of affection physically, and I wondered if he was worried someone would see, or if public displays of affection just were not Wade's thing. Not that he needed to show affection, since I wasn't really sure if we were a thing or not.

Once outside, I slid into the back seat of Archer's SUV and said hi when I saw Ruthie sitting in the front passenger seat.

"Sorry about your car situation," Ruthie expressed, and I looked over to the rearview mirror, hoping to see Archer's face to let me know how much he'd told Ruthie about the situation.

"She knows about the tracker and your ex," he explained, and I wasn't sure if I was relieved I didn't have to lie to her or embarrassed that she knew about it. "I'm not in the habit of telling strangers your business, but I need her to know so she can keep an eye out if he calls or comes around the office."

It made sense, but I also didn't like the thought of Randall coming around. It frustrated me that he was doing this and wouldn't just leave me alone.

"I also have a car, Ellie, so if you need to borrow it, just let me know and I can just steal Archer's car for the day, or I can pick you up and drive you myself," Ruthie offered, which was very sweet.

"First of all, she's not borrowing your car because she isn't allowed to drive anywhere by herself. Wade, Vince, or I will drive her. Oh, and Ellie," Archer paused. "Word of advice. Do not let Ruthie drive you anywhere," he said, his warning laced with a bit of humor.

"Oh my God, Grandma. You act like you're a better driver than me," Ruthie bit back.

"I *am* a better driver. Unlike you, I don't drive like I'm auditioning for Fast & Furious," he said snidely but while also grinning.

I realized two things at that moment. One, Ruthie was not the quiet little mouse I'd thought she was. Two, these two were ribbing each other— not in a mean, cynical way, but rather how siblings would tease each other. How Jack and I used to before he left for the Army.

"My driving is just...peppy and efficient," Ruthie defended. "I get us places quickly, unlike your turtle driving."

"Speed racing is more like it, with a mild heart attack included," Archer added. "Ellie, I will get you there in one piece, unlike this one, who curbs sidewalks like it's her second job."

"That doesn't count," Ruthie defended. "That construction worker put that cone too far out into the other lane. I had no choice but to drive a few inches over the curb. Admit it, it was a little thrilling."

"If by thrilling you mean terrifying, then yes, *very* thrilling." He laughed.

"If I drive Ellie, she won't have to grip the door handle for dear life and will actually make it to the gym in one piece," he stated and looked at me through the rearview mirror with a smirk on his face.

Ruthie huffed, and I laughed. This reminded me so much of how Jack and I used to quibble when we were kids, and I missed it. I missed him.

Archer must have sensed my mood turning.

"Ellie, we're just kidding, by the way. No need to be worried," he said in a softer tone.

"Oh no, I'm okay," I explained to them both. "This just reminded me of the spats my brother and I used to have as kids, and I realized how much I missed him and being able to razz him. You guys fight like siblings. I take it you've known each other for a long time. How did you meet?"

For what seemed like a simple question, the mood in the car definitely shifted. They both went quiet and looked at each other. Archer spoke up first.

"We met in Vegas, and when I was packing up to move here to start the business with the guys, Ruthie was also looking for a change and decided to move here too," he said while glancing over at Ruthie a few times. "She had the skills necessary to work with us, and we needed a receptionist so the timing all worked out."

"Plus, my grandpa lives in Georgia," Ruthie divulged.

I sensed that wasn't the whole story, but I didn't want to press. Maybe I could ask Ruthie about it later when we were alone and see if she would open up.

The rest of the car ride was filled with more generic conversation about how Archer was going to be on the other side of the gym and for us to let him know when we were done.

We walked into the gym, and Ruthie helped me get signed up for the class. Then, we headed to the locker room to drop our bags off.

Ruthie took off her ring and earrings and shared that sometimes the jewelry gets in the way, so she doesn't like to wear her rings or earrings to class.

"Right," she said, clapping her hands together once and putting on a determined face. "Now let's go kick some ass to make ourselves feel better."

I laughed and followed her into class.

An hour later, I was sufficiently worn out, sweating from head to toe—but I also felt more empowered. The class combined kickboxing, taekwondo, and other self-defense tactics designed to teach basic self-defense while also providing an intense workout.

Ruthie and I showered and changed in the locker room then met Archer out front. We all decided to eat dinner at the Mexican restaurant across the street.

"We just burned all those calories. Might as well put them all right back on again with chips and queso," Ruthie remarked.

"I'm not sure you understand the concept of a work-out," Archer informed her with a grin as she rolled her eyes at him.

We got a booth and sat down, but Archer went to the bar instead, mentioning that Wade was going to meet him there. Honestly, this was better because I wanted to talk to Ruthie, and it would be ideal if Archer wasn't sitting right next to us.

"Thanks for inviting me. I needed that," I told Ruthie.

"You're welcome," she replied. "I hope I wasn't too forward by texting you the other night and inviting you. Archer said sometimes I can be a little blunt."

I chuckled a little at the look on her face that clearly conveyed that she didn't want to admit that she agreed with him.

"I have to admit, when I first met you, I thought you were a quiet little introvert," I shared.

"I can be," she remarked. "I'm protective of Archer and the guys because they gave me this awesome job, and I know the security business deals a lot with privacy, so I tend to seem that way when I'm in *office mode*. I'm sorry if I came off as rude when I first met you. I didn't know you were Jack's sister. Wade just mentioned you were some new hire from the pub. I didn't make the connection until later."

Her explanation made sense. I told her not to worry about it. My move here to Georgia was kind of last minute, so I doubted Archer and Vince had been given much notice either.

"You seem in a good mood today, given everything that has happened the last few days," Ruthie noted, then paused and leaned in closer. "You hangin' in there?"

I sighed thinking back to what a pain Randall had been in my life the past year and how I hated that I couldn't just move on.

"You don't have to talk about it if you don't want to." She held up her hands as if to tell me there was no pressure.

"I don't mind. Honestly, it would be kind of nice talking to someone about it," I explained to her. "My friend Katie from back in Tennessee is great to talk to, but she doesn't know the guys like you do, so you may have more insight, which would be helpful. Though, if we talk about this, I might need something a little stronger than a Dr. Pepper."

As if she'd heard us, our waitress walked up right at that moment to take our order.

"Let's get some stronger drinks, then. Archer can drop us both off so neither of us has to drive," she declared, and we both ordered a margarita and our meals.

I started at the beginning, telling her all the details about Randall. Her facial expressions changed from anger to sadness to sympathy and then to a murderous glare, but she never interrupted or pressed me for extra information. She just accepted what I was willing to give, and for that I was so grateful.

"I just feel like an idiot sometimes for not seeing him

for the monster he is," I told her. "Especially since my brother and gran clearly saw something I didn't."

"Forgive yourself for not knowing what you didn't know before you learned it," Ruthie said to me and then paused. "That's my favorite quote from Maya Angelou. I find it's a good reminder to not be so hard on yourself for past mistakes in life."

That quote really hit home for me. I realized she was right. I needed to do that. Forgive myself for the mistake of being with Randall when I didn't know the kind of monster he was. The quote made me wonder about Ruthie's past. Did she too have a rough past? She must have seen the question and concern on my face, because she spoke up again.

"I promise to tell you my story too, but let me talk to Archer first," she said quietly. "It involves a police case he worked on, and I'm not sure I'm allowed to share all of the details."

I'd like for her to share and be able to help her like she was helping me, but I also understood what she was saying. Hopefully we could become good friends and she would confide in me when she was ready.

Just then, she looked up and to my side and produced a small smile.

"How did self-defense class go?"

I heard Wade's smooth voice before I saw him appear to my side of the booth.

"Are you two considered ninjas now? If I steal one of your tortilla chips, are you going to make me regret it?"

He had a big smirk on his face as he joked with us. He'd changed from earlier and was now wearing jeans, an Atlanta Falcons T-shirt, and a baseball cap on backwards. He looked so good, and he clearly wasn't even trying. I felt my face heating as Ruthie replied back to him.

"Touch my chips and you'll have to sleep with one eye open." She glared at him, but then smiled to let him know she was messing with him.

He chuckled then put his hand on my shoulder and gave a small squeeze.

"You ladies enjoy your dinner," he uttered then walked over to the bar to meet Archer.

I looked back at Ruthie, and her eyes were wide, staring at me. While she said nothing, the look on her face spoke volumes, telling me she didn't miss the soft touch to my shoulder.

Her eyebrows rose as she smirked. I knew my face was likely turning pink. She chuckled a little at my clear embarrassment.

Maybe it was because my brain was fried from everything the last few days of dealing with Randall, or maybe I was just tired from the intense workout at self-defense class, or maybe both, but instead of opening my mouth to tell her it was no big deal, I ended up blurting out the truth instead.

"We had sex!" I said quickly then gasped in disbelief that I'd just told her that.

Her eyes widened at first in shock, but then she gave me a small smile. I knew my face must have been bright red by now, so I took my hands and covered it, leaning down into them on the table.

"Don't leave me hanging!" she replied.

I sighed and realized in for a penny, in for a pound.

"It happened the night after we went to his family's house for lunch," I told her about the building sexual tension with him the last few weeks.

I explained that I had woken up hearing Wade talk in his sleep, though I don't disclose any details about the night terrors or his PTSD. I told her all the other details though.

She listened intently without saying much except to laugh a little when I explained to her that we'd been sleeping at his place because he felt it broke some weird bro-code to sleep with me in Jack's bed.

After detailing everything, I exhaled, then grabbed my margarita and took a very long swig—or three.

Her face changed from smiling and clearly entertained to one of concern.

"You don't seem happy about this," she said before leaning in close and speaking quietly. "Was the sex not good?"

"Oh gosh, no, the sex was great," I clarified but also talking low so the other tables didn't hear us. "I'm pretty sure I had an out-of-body experience that night."

She chuckled, smiling.

"Then why the long face?" she asked.

"I just don't want to rush into anything, you know?" I tried to point out. I explained how with everything with

Randall, moving to a new state, and trying to enroll in school, I didn't need to get caught up in anything complicated right now.

"I get that, trust me. I just moved here and am trying to do the same in terms of getting the new version of me started," she told me. "But you also can't help when the timing is right. Why don't you just take it slow and see where things go? If it works out, then great, it works out."

She made it seem so simple, but there were layers of complication with Wade compared to other guys.

"But if it doesn't work out, I don't want it to be awkward with Jack and the security business," I rationalized.

"I get that, but you also shouldn't hold back from something you want just in the off chance something might go bad," she said, and I knew what she was saying was right, but it was hard to get my brain to understand. "And in the short term, at least you get to have some amazing sex."

We both smiled and chuckled, looking up just in time to see our food had arrived.

The rest of the conversation was easygoing, and I decided I really liked Ruthie and wanted to make a point to hang out with her more.

After dinner, both Archer and Wade made their way over to our booth, informing us that they paid the bill and it was time to get us home before we "drank ourselves into a stupor." I just chuckled at the comment, but Ruthie took personal offense and had no problem lighting into

Archer as we left the building, which just made me chuckle more.

It made no sense for me to ride back with Archer since he and Ruthie lived in the same building going one way, and Wade and I lived in the same building in the opposite direction. In a brief reprieve from arguing with Archer, Ruthie turned to me, wished me a good night, and winked at me, holding her thumbs up— okay, maybe she was a little drunker than I'd thought.

Wade met me at the passenger door to his SUV and opened it for me. He walked around and got into his side before speaking. "How'd your evening go? Did you enjoy the class with Ruthie?"

I smiled, nodding. "The class was fun, even though some of the moves were intense and thoroughly kicked my butt. The dinner and drinks helped me recover though." I smiled even bigger. "I think Ruthie and I are becoming really good friends."

"That's good, babe. She seems nice," he said, and my heart fluttered a little bit at the sound of him calling me babe.

He'd only said that once before, but I thought it was a fluke. I didn't quite know what to make of it now that he had said it a second time.

"Umm...yeah, she is, and it's fun watching her and Archer together because they bicker like siblings," I told him. "It reminds me of Jack and me when we were younger."

"Yeah, I don't know the whole story there, but I do know they knew each other back in Vegas," he divulged.

The rest of the car ride was filled with us explaining about our days, and it felt like a conversation you would have with a partner or a really good friend, not just someone you were sleeping with. As much as I would have liked to ask him about that topic, I didn't exactly know how to do it without it being awkward, so I just let it go for now and enjoyed the comfortable talk.

We got back to the building and headed up to his apartment. After cleaning up and changing, I found him in bed watching a game on TV. I got into the bed next to him and pulled out my phone to text Katie and email my brother to check in on him. Feeling tired after class, I set my phone down and decided I would just watch whatever Wade had on the TV and let it put me to sleep, since sports usually did that for me. I settled in, and Wade reached over and pulled me into his side. He wasn't really looking at me, but his left arm was on my thigh, which he had now draped over his leg. His right hand was in my hair, just slowly fingering through the ends, and it felt so good.

"That feels nice," I told him.

"Yeah?" he asked, and I nodded in return.

His eyes were now on me, and the hand on my thigh started sliding up.

His mouth came down to kiss me softly on my lips.

"That feels nice too." I gave him a smile, and hoped he would take the hint.

He grinned at me lasciviously, then kissed me again. That kiss quickly turned heated, which led to other things that felt nice.

Two orgasms later, I was even more tired than I was before, but also very happy. I realized I could get used to this. And that thought scared me.

16

ELLIE

Wade and Tammy had redone the schedule so I was now working more bar shifts rather than waiting tables, since I would always be behind the bar with someone else— whether that was Tammy, Wade, Sam, or whoever— and they would be close. I wasn't sure it was needed anymore because Randall hadn't called again since Tammy told him I no longer worked here and we moved my car. The plan was working, but Wade and the guys still wanted me to be protected at all times until they could "check a few more things." They never divulged what those things were, but I assumed that was what badass security people specialized in, so I didn't push.

Wade and I still hung out most nights, unless I was working the late shift, but even then, he would come get me and walk me back to the apartment after my shift. We ate meals together, watched movies, and, yes, shared more amazing sex. The lines were definitely blurred, but I wasn't sure how to bring it up, and Wade didn't try to bring it up either.

One morning this week, I finally talked myself into bringing the topic up casually over breakfast, but he took a phone call from Vince, who informed him he'd just moved my car back. Wade explained that the tracker on my car had been removed and was now currently on Jack's car sitting in Archer's apartment complex parking lot. This way they could keep an eye on it while still giving Randall the impression I had moved in case he was still tracking it. This meant I finally had my car back. I was so excited that I forgot to ask Wade about where we stood in terms of being a couple or just having casual sex. I always felt so guilty having to ask one of the guys to go with me for groceries or to the store, and I really needed to go clothes shopping.

With my newfound freedom of transportation, I took off on some errands, which Wade told me was fine as long as I told them where I was going and agreed to share my location on my phone with all the guys. It also felt good to be able to offer to drive when Ruthie and I hung out instead of always having her drive. Especially since Archer was right—Ruthie was a speed demon behind the wheel.

A few days after I got my car back, I was getting in so I could drive over to one of the nearby college campuses and check it out for next semester. As I slid into the driver's seat, I noticed the seat was pushed back really far and all of my mirrors were nowhere near where they needed to be. It startled me a little, but I realized one of the guys must have just borrowed the car and forgotten to move everything back.

A few days after that, I turned on my car and the radio was on full blast. Deafeningly loud music shot from the speakers to the point where even after I turned it down, my ears were still ringing for what felt like an entire minute. I hardly ever listened to music in my car, preferring audiobooks or podcasts, so I was very confused but chocked it up to maybe bumping the buttons on accident.

The final straw for me was when I went out to my car to grab my umbrella from the passenger seat floor where I left it and saw one of those green tree car air fresheners hanging from my rearview mirror. I sat frozen in the seat for a moment, realizing that I would not have put that in there. I preferred the ones you clipped to your car's vents, not the kind that hung from the mirror, distracting you as they swung. A chill ran through me as I remembered that Randall loved those air freshener trees in his car. My stomach churned with dread as I pulled out my phone and called Wade, who answered immediately.

"Hey, babe," he answered, and I went right into it.

"Did you put an air freshener in my car?" I asked him.

"What?" he asked.

"An air freshener," I explained. "Like the ones that look like a Christmas tree hanging from your rearview mirror. Did you or one of the guys put one in my car?"

"No, I didn't, and I can't see why Vince or Archer

would have done that. What's going on," he started to say with more of an alertness in his voice. "Where are you?"

"I'm in the parking lot on the side over next to the hair salon," I explained to him.

"Get out of the car and go into the salon and stay in there until I come for you," he told me sternly. "I'm walking out of the building now."

I agreed and stayed on the phone with him as I walked up to the salon. There were several complexes near the pub and Ranger Shield Security that were mixed use, businesses on the main floor and apartments on the upper floors. I liked to park over by the salon, which was across the street diagonally to the pub, because they had more spots that were under the shade of trees, so my car wasn't a thousand degrees when I got inside. I walked into the salon, pretending to just browse the hair products on the far wall while I waited for Wade. I saw him and Vince walk up to my car, and I made my way outside.

They started to inspect the car, inside and out, before Vince spoke.

"Has this ever happened before?" He sounded concerned and angry.

"No, but there have been some other weird occur-rences lately," I said and then told them both about my seat and mirrors being moved, as well as the radio incident.

Wade's eyes twitched, and I could see his jaw start to strain as I explained the other happenings.

They looked at each other and said a few words that

sounded like code and didn't mean anything to me, before looking back at me. I realized I was about to lose some of my car freedom all over again.

Technically, the guys didn't say I couldn't drive it anymore, but they did make me park my car right in front of the entrance to Ranger Shield, where it would be covered by their security cameras. Wade informed me I *must* park it there from now on, and I had to tell them if anything else out of the ordinary happened. No exceptions.

"Better safe than sorry," Wade remarked, his expression serious. "We can't take any chances after what happened."

I agreed, especially since this latest incident had me a little spooked myself. Ruthie even called me later to tell me that Archer was making her park her car next to mine.

"Hey, just got the memo from Archer. We get to be car neighbors now," Ruthie joked, likely trying to cheer me up.

I felt guilty that my problems were spreading to other people.

"Sorry about that. I didn't mean to drag you into this mess."

"Don't worry about it," she countered. "Just let me know if you need anything. We're all in this together. The guys too."

"I'll bake you all some cookies," I offered.

"You think Archer eats cookies?" Ruthie shot back. "He's basically a robot. But go ahead and make them anyway—I'll just eat his. Actually, make some for all the guys. None of them will eat them because they're obsessed with keeping their bodies in tip-top shape, but it'll be a nice gesture. Plus, then we can eat them all ourselves."

I couldn't help but chuckle, but guilt still gnawed at me. My problems with Randall were creating inconveniences for everyone around me, and I hated it.

17

ELLIE

Ruthie and I were scheduled to have lunch today down the street from the office at a sushi restaurant. She and I had been making a habit of going to lunch or dinner together and getting to know each other better.

Ruthie even confided in me about her past—and how she met Archer in Las Vegas.

"After my mom died when I was fourteen, things went downhill fast," Ruthie began. "My dad always wanted sons, and only sons. He basically hated me, so my older brother Jason ended up raising me. By the time I was twenty, I'd saved enough to move out, but Jason's friend Mal wouldn't leave me alone. He always sent me roses and jewelry, which creeped me out. Turns out, the jewelry was stolen. When I turned it into the police, I inadvertently exposed my family's pawn shop, which was selling the stolen goods. In turn, I landed my dad and brother in jail."

I stared at her, wide-eyed. "That's insane."

"It didn't stop there," she said sadly. "One of their associates broke into my apartment and nearly killed me. Archer was the responding officer and suggested I move for my safety. Since my grandpa lived here, it seemed like a natural place. That, and Archer offered me a job."

While Ruthie's story wasn't the same as mine, we both knew what it was like to be haunted by people who wouldn't leave us alone. It was an odd thing to bond over, but we did. And since neither of us knew many people here, we found a strange comfort in having each other.

She was also really great to talk to about Wade—which lately was becoming more complicated since I was still staying with him in his apartment, but we hadn't really had any conversations about where we stood or what we were doing.

Needless to say, I was looking forward to lunch with Ruthie today so I could pick her brain a little.

I walked out of the elevator and turned right into the main entrance to the front lobby, where Ruthie was sitting behind her desk. She was on the phone and looked at me while holding up her finger, indicating she just needed a minute. I gave her a thumbs-up and sat down in one of the chairs by the front windows. Ruthie said goodbye and hung up the phone before turning to me.

"The phrase 'the customer is always right' is definitely not a one-size-fits-all rule," Ruthie sighed, rolling her eyes.

Having worked in the service industry for several years, I understood her frustration.

"Can you give me a few minutes to sort some things for Vince really quick?" she asked me. "That was a thirty-five-minute waste of a call I did not have time for, and Vince needed these reports within the hour."

"Sure, or we can order, and I can just go pick the food up while you finish up and bring it back here, and we can eat in the fancy conference room," I told her, because I honestly didn't care where we ate. I just wanted to catch up with her, and I knew Mondays were chaotic for her.

"Are you sure? You don't need to walk there. We can just get delivery," Ruthie countered, looking unsure. "I know the guys don't want you walking anywhere by yourself."

"They removed the tracker from my car, and we haven't had any calls lately, so Wade said I could have a little more freedom. I'm just going across the street."

Ruthie hesitated, then looked at me with sadness and guilt in her eyes, and I knew she must be feeling bad for having to adjust our lunch, but I honestly didn't care where we ate as long as we got to chat.

"This time of day, it would be quicker for me to walk over and pick it up myself," I explained. "Let's just place the order, and I'll walk over and get it in a few minutes and bring it back here."

I pulled up the app on my phone and typed in my order. When I went to hand it to her, she handed me a small box she pulled from her purse.

"Since you liked mine so much, I got you one too," Ruthie uttered.

I opened the box to find a charm of boxing gloves, similar to the one I had complimented her on during a shift at the bar one night.

"Now we match, just like sisters," she said, her jaw twitching slightly. "I got you a yellow pair since I know you're not a pink person like me." She smiled weakly.

Her voice wavered slightly, and I could see emotion in her eyes that I couldn't quite pinpoint. Ruthie had once mentioned she only had a brother, like me, so I chalked it up to this gesture making her sentimental.

"This one can be added to your charm necklace here," she said. "I know you said your grandma gave you that necklace, but I figure this can be a new charm to represent a new phase in your life."

I smiled at her and thanked her sincerely. The gesture was incredibly thoughtful, and, I loved her idea of how it symbolized my fresh start here in Georgia. She reached into her desk drawer and handed me the tools to attach it to my necklace. She appeared oddly insistent I put it on before I left, so to make her happy, I added it on and thanked her again. It really was a beautiful charm.

Afterward, I walked over to the restaurant to pick up our order. While I waited by the register, I suddenly felt like someone was staring at me. It was a weird feeling, but my body was already on alert because I was by myself, and I knew the guys would frown at me for coming here alone. I turned and glanced around the restaurant, but nothing seemed out of the ordinary, and no one even seemed to be paying me any attention. Still, I couldn't help but shake that creepy feeling.

"Order for Ellie!" the cashier called out.

I grabbed my order and made my way to the door just as a sharp jolt startled me. Someone bumped into me hard enough to make me stumble back.

"Oh, I'm sorry," I said instinctively, looking up.

The man before me was older, maybe in his fifties, with a face etched in harsh lines and eyes that held nothing kind. He didn't say a word—just stared at me, unblinking, his expression cold and unsettling.

"Excuse me," I said, trying to move around him to the exit.

He didn't budge, his gaze tracked me like a predator sizing up prey.

"Watch yourself," he finally said, his voice low and menacing.

Heart pounding, I pushed past him quickly and turned around to look, but he was already gone, as though he'd vanished into thin air.

Just to be on the safe side, though, I quickened my pace across the street. By the time I reached the safety of the front office, I practically burst through the door.

"Are you ok? Did you run here?" she asked, looking a little worried.

"I'm fine." I didn't want to share everything with her because I was pretty sure I was just being paranoid about the guy. "Some rude guy just bumped into me on the way out."

"I knew you shouldn't have gone over there alone!" she scolded, shaking her head.

"It's not a big deal. Let's just eat." I told her

I wasn't sure she believed me, but she didn't call me out on it.

We enjoyed our lunch and chatted for an hour about a new book we'd both started reading and how we wanted to try out some of the newer hiking trails at the nearby Chattahoochee National Forest. We made plans for the following weekend when we both had a day off.

After lunch, I returned to my apartment to shower and change for my shift. That evening, I was waiting tables since we had two people call in sick. It wasn't as fun as working the bar with Tammy but usually earned me better tips. Plus, Wade mentioned he was working behind the bar for a few hours tonight because Sam had plans, so he couldn't come in until after the dinner rush.

During the dinner rush, I approached one of my booths, which had been seated with a new party of four at it. The semi-circle booths in the back had high sides, making it hard to see who was seated. As I got closer, I noticed the older woman sitting on the end looked vaguely familiar, but I couldn't place her right away. As I got closer, I saw all four women look up and smile at me, and I realized this table was full of Wade's family, minus his dad.

"Ellie, so good to see you," his mom said with a smile. "What a coincidence we got you as our waitress. How wonderful!"

The rest of the table chuckled, and I realized maybe she'd seen me and asked for me on purpose. I smiled at that thought.

"Well, I'm happy you're all here," I told them. "Now let me see if I can remember everyone's names." I paused, thinking in my head. "Willa and Whitney," I said pointing to his two sisters sitting on the right. "And you're Wendy." I pointed to his mom but then paused. "Hmmm, they all called you Nana, so I'm not sure I remember your name, but I'm guessing it starts with a W like everyone else's," I joked.

"Nonsense. All that name weirdness started with my daughter." She waved her hand around. "My name is Carol, but you can call me Nana too if that's easier." She smiled at me, and I instantly missed my own gran.

I got their drink and food orders and put them in, occasionally going back to check on them, but the place was busy, so I didn't have much time to chat with them over the next twenty minutes.

I was making my way to one of my other tables with some appetizers when I noticed Wade was now at the booth talking with his family. He didn't look very happy. Was there something wrong with their food? Had they needed a refill? Once I set the food down on my current table, I started to make my way back to Wade's family's table to see if they needed something. As I got closer, I heard them talking, but then Wade turned to me and stopped talking. His face was unreadable but still slightly grumpy.

"Is everything okay? Do you guys need anything?" I asked his family.

"We're fine, dear," his mom said. "Wade here apparently doesn't like it when we come to visit. Supposedly we embarrass him."

"You aren't here to visit me, and we both know it," Wade said, staring at his mom, who appeared to be unaffected by his glare. "You called Tammy to ask when Ellie was working tables then came in on that very night and specifically asked to be seated in her section so you could ambush her."

"Well, Wade, if you weren't dragging your feet, we wouldn't have to do the ambushing, now would we?" His grandma chuckled and raised her eyebrows.

"Besides, Ellie seems happy to see us," Willa said. "And we plan to leave a generous tip for her emotional support expenses now that she has to live with you."

Every woman at the table just grinned, but I felt my face turning bright red. They knew we were living together?

"You're all pains in my ass, you know that?" Wade grumbled.

All four women chuckled at his grumpiness, and it made me smile.

Wade turned to me and spoke softer as he put his right hand around the back of my neck and shoulder. "I'm headed out. I'll be back at the end of your shift to come get you and head back to the apartment."

He leaned in to kiss me on my temple, his hand slowly moving down my back and slightly squeezed my hip, and then he turned and walked away.

He'd kissed me. In public! I knew it wasn't on the lips, but it was definitely something you wouldn't do to just any coworker, and there were people around. In fact, when I looked up, Beth was staring at me with a look on her face that clearly said, "Sure you two are *just* friends."

I didn't realize I was standing there frozen for a few seconds until Wade's mom spoke.

"Aww, that was so cute," she said, smiling at me.

"Who knew the big brute had a soft side," Whitney said, chuckling.

"You two are cute together," his grandma said. "You will make such beautiful great-grandbabies for me."

The rest of the table all laughed while my face continued to turn even redder and my eyes widened. Not knowing what to say to that comment, I tried to go back to waitress mode.

"Can I get you guys anything else?" I asked.

"Just the check, my dear," Wade's mom said with a huge smile on her face still.

They left about fifteen minutes later, and yes, they gave me a huge tip. Trying not to think too much about what just happened, I moved over to my other three tables to check on everyone and ask about refills. As I walked over to the bar to put in an order for another table,

Tammy was waiting for me and staring at me as I walked toward her with a big smile on her face.

"I see you decided to go with the 'have more fun' option." She shot me a knowing look as I typed in my drink order and sighed.

"I don't know what is happening exactly," I told her.

"Ask him," Tammy said, like it was the simplest thing in the world.

"It's not that simple," I tried to explain to her.

"Honey, men are simple creatures. Most of the time you don't have to ask a guy what they're thinking because it's usually only about their job, sports, food, and sex, or some combination of those four," she said as she turned to make my drink order. "But if you need clarification, just ask. Especially with a guy like Wade, who is gonna give it to you straight."

I didn't have anything else to say because I didn't know how to respond to that, so I just stood there.

"Alright, here you go," she said, handing me my drinks. "Just talk to him, sweetheart. This doesn't have to be any more complicated than you want it to be."

I nodded, knowing she was right, but still nervous. The rest of the night was uneventful and seemed to go by very quickly.

I was cleaning up one of my last tables when I saw Wade come in the front door. He saw me and started to walk over to me. His mood was definitely better than when he was here earlier talking with his family.

"Hey babe, I'll be in the back office working on the

schedule. Just come get me when you're done," he said, winking at me and then walking back to the office.

Beth walked up next to me and had a weird grin on her face.

"*Babe?*" she said beside me, almost shocked. "Yeah, you're *just* friends." She snorted then walked back over to her tables.

Why had he called me that in public? I knew we'd been staying together, but that was because of Randall. Was it because of the sex? Maybe Tammy was right and we needed to have a talk. I didn't need anything else complicated in my life right now, especially a man. A good-looking man too.

I cleaned the rest of my tables, closed out at the bar, and said goodbye to everyone as I walked back to the office. The door was open, so I stepped into the doorway. Wade was sitting there at his desk writing things down on a piece of paper. When he didn't look up, I took the opportunity to study him. He really was incredibly handsome. He had on a fitted Army green T-shirt that showed off his upper arm muscles and some of his tattoos. His hair looked a little damp, like he'd showered right before he came here but hadn't dried it all the way. The muscles in his forearm flexed as he wrote things down, and I started to feel myself flush thinking of how good those arms had felt wrapped around me.

"You keep staring at me like that, and I'm gonna take you right there on that couch. We won't make it upstairs." Wade's comment startled me out of my thoughts.

His words flowed right through me, making my skin heat up from the inside out.

"Ellie," he all but growled at me. "Grab your bag. Let's go."

He stood from his desk, and I turned around quickly to grab my purse from my cubby in the breakroom. With my purse in hand, I turned to see Wade in the doorway, but just as we were about to leave, Sam came walking toward us.

"Hey Ellie, some guy left this for you on one of your tables, said he forgot to leave a tip earlier," Sam said, handing me an envelope of some kind.

I thanked him and lifted the lip of the envelope to open it. It had a folded-up piece of paper inside, which I opened.

Confused, I looked back at the piece of paper and unfolded it, and I suddenly got light-headed. It felt like all my blood rushed to my feet, and I knew my face had gone bone-white. Inside was a very simple handwritten message.

"Whores don't belong here! That man does not belong to you. Do not put your filthy hands on another man. You don't belong here. You belong in Tennessee. You will be going home whether you like it or not."

Wade must have seen the reaction on my face, because the piece of paper was taken from my hands, but I didn't remember much in that moment because my mind started spinning and I felt myself getting dizzy, scared, and angry all at the same time.

I felt Wade grab my arms and set me down on the bench and heard him talking to someone before he crouched down in front of me and put his hands on my face.

"Ellie, baby look at me," he said softly to me. I looked up at him but didn't say anything. "You're safe."

"He knows I'm here, and he knows about you," I said as I looked in his eyes and started to panic.

"Breathe, baby. Just breathe. We don't know it was him personally. He could have gotten someone else to do it," Wade said and that got my attention.

"You think so?" I asked softly.

"Diego is upstairs in the office still, so I'm having him check the cameras to see what this guy looks like," he said calmly, though I was sure he was only calm for my benefit. He got up and walked back to the doorway.

"Hey Chuck," he yelled down the hall to the kitchen area, where Chuck was still cooking. "Need a favor. Can you go get Sam and tell him to come back here ASAP? Thanks."

He turned and came back to me, squatting down to my level. His eyes were looking me over, assessing me, likely to see if I was going to break down. He put his hands on the top of my thighs, and his thumbs rubbed softly across my jeans, almost soothingly. This motion oddly calmed me, and I felt my panic attack starting to subside.

"I'm okay," I told him. He stared at me as if trying to assess whether I was telling the truth or not.

"What's up, boss?" Sam came into the doorway then glanced down at Wade in front of me, with me probably still a little pale. "Everything okay?"

"Can you describe the man who gave you the envelope to give to Ellie? Recognize him?" Wade spoke as he stood, staying close to me.

"Uh, no, didn't recognize him," Sam said, scratching his head. "Honestly, the dude kept his head down, just mumbled he forgot to tip you, and he dropped the envelope off at the bar. I was mid-drink pour, but I grabbed it so no one else would help themselves to it. Dude was old-lookin' though. My guess, late fifties or sixties. Looked rough too. Like he hadn't showered in a few days, maybe even homeless."

"Right, thanks. You can head back to the bar," Wade said to Sam.

Sam nodded but hesitated walking away. He probably sensed something was up but also knew he was leaving the bar to Chuck and needed to get back.

Wade made another call to Diego then hustled me safely out of the pub and up the stairs to his apartment.

"Go ahead and get changed, babe. Do your routine, and I'll meet you in the bedroom in a minute," he declared, brokering no room for argument.

I could tell he was angry, though he was trying to keep calm, likely for my sake. I was too tired and angry myself to argue with him, so I went back to the bathroom to wash my face and brush my teeth. I really was wiped from a long shift, and then the letter nonsense took the last bit of energy I had. I was walking back into the bedroom, and I could hear he was on the phone. Likely calling Archer or Vince, or both, to update them.

I couldn't wait to get to a point in time when these men were not spending all their time fixing my problems. I couldn't wait to not have to deal with Randall at all. I growled low in my throat. I hated that man for not leaving me alone. I just wanted to go to school, have a job I enjoyed, see my brother again, spend time with friends, and just have a normal, quiet life. I tried to still my racing brain and focus on the task of getting ready for bed.

I'd just finished changing into my pajamas when Wade came into view, standing in the doorway. His face was blank, but I focused on his arms, which were stretched out to the top of the door frame. His muscles were on full display.

The back of my mind still raced from the letter and Randall, but at that moment, Wade looked so gorgeous, it was hard to ignore. His thick, corded muscles fully flexed as though he was using the door frame to support himself. It was total arm porn, and I bit my lip, enjoying the sight. With his arms up, his tee now bared a hint of skin over his stomach, and a peak of his sculpted abs were on display. I looked down even further, and I could see the evidence of a bulge in his pants. God, what that man could do with that part of his body. I'd obviously seen it in use, but Wade was more of the take charge, "we do it my way" kind of guy, so I hadn't really been able to explore that particular part of his anatomy in great detail with my hands or mouth yet. I realized in that moment, I wished I could.

"Ellie, my eyes are up here," Wade teased.

I grinned back at him, knowing he'd caught me looking, but I didn't care. His face softened and he started to walk toward me.

"We need to talk about tonight," he said softly. "You doing okay?"

"Surprisingly yes," I told him, and I meant it. I realized that even though the letter had spooked me, Wade was a calming presence and had brought me back to the here and now, where I knew I was safe.

"You sure?" he asked, cupping my face.

I nodded and moved my body into his, so we were touching from chest to thigh. Wrapping my arms around his torso, I hugged him closer.

"I am," I said as I tilted my head back a little and looked into his eyes. "We don't need to talk about it. I really am okay. I'm peeved about the note and angry that Randall won't leave me alone, but there's nothing I can do about it right this moment, so no sense worrying or focusing all my time on it. There are other things I'd rather do instead."

I moved my hands from around him back to the front of his chest and slid them slowly up and down. I could see in his eyes he was unsure of what to do. So, I leaned forward and kissed him, making the decision for both of us.

It was just a soft kiss, and at first, he just let me take

control. I opened my mouth and put my tongue on his lips, and he opened for me.

That was when the kiss turned heated, and his hands, once gently cupping my cheeks, slid down to my neck. He tilted my head to intensify the connection, but I could sense he was holding back. He broke the kiss briefly, resting his forehead against mine. He probably thought I should be an emotional wreck after the letter and didn't want to push me. But I wasn't. Being in his arms made me feel safer than I ever had. If he was going to hold back, though, I decided to take control and do what I wanted.

I pulled back slightly, meeting his gaze for a moment before dropping to my knees in front of him. My hands found his belt, and I began unfastening it.

"Babe," he uttered, trying to stop my hands from undoing the button on his jeans.

"No, Wade, I need this, and I want to do this," I explained to him in the most stern, no-nonsense voice I could muster while lowering the zipper on his pants and continuing on with my mission.

He let out a low, calm protest, gripping my wrists to stop me. "Not sure I want my dick in your mouth while you're angry and upset."

Before I could respond, he growled, "Later," and pulled me back to my feet.

He kissed me again, harder this time. The kiss was fierce, almost primal, as though we were channeling the adrenaline from everything that had just happened into this moment. He walked me backward toward the bed, breaking the kiss only when I felt it against the back of my knees.

Dazed, I heard the faint rustling sound and glanced down to see him rolling on a condom. Seconds later, he was inside me.

"You feel so damn good," he muttered, his voice low and gravelly.

He was pumping in and out of me frantically, as though he couldn't control himself. He leaned down and sucked hard on my left nipple, while simultaneously rolling my right nipple between his fingers.

My first orgasm was barely a memory as my next one began to crash over me. I cried out his name again as pure bliss rolled through my entire body.

"Ellie," he groaned as his body jerked through his release.

We lay there for what seemed like a long time, but undoubtably was likely just minutes. We were both still breathing heavy, and he rolled to the side. He kissed my forehead as he got up to go dispose of the condom. When he came back, he curled me so that I was laying half on top of him while he was on his back. Almost instantly, I was asleep, completely forgetting everything that happened earlier in the evening and forgetting that I wanted to talk with him.

18

WADE

Ellie's brother Jack was finally stateside. He messaged us all a few days ago to let us know he was back on U.S. soil and currently on base, finishing his debriefing and paper-work to officially transition out of military life. If every-thing went smoothly, he would be flying home to Atlanta tomorrow, and would arrive around dinnertime.

Most of our communication with him up to that point had been through quick texts here and there, but today, we planned to talk with him on a group call with Archer and Vince to get him up to speed about Ellie's stalker. Due to the incident last night, Archer, Vince, and I had decided to move up the timeline for our plan.

The three of us, along with Diego, were sitting in Vince's office up on the second floor of our building. The four of us had just finalized our plans to deal with Ellie's ex and were waiting for Jack to call.

Vince's phone rang, and he put it on speaker as he answered.

"Vinnie!" Jack's voice bellowed.

"Hey man, good to hear your voice back on U.S. soil for a change," Vince said.

"Same, and I'm happy to *not* be eating MREs day in and day out, that's for damn sure," Jack joked.

Vince, Diego, and I grunted in agreement, knowing how much a real meal could mean after those pre-packaged military rations for so long.

"Well, just don't do the cooking yourself," Vince teased. "We don't need you dying as soon as you're back because you poisoned yourself with your own cooking."

None of us were great cooks by any means, but Jack was by far the worst. That man couldn't make a piece of toast to save his life.

"Yeah, yeah, assholes," Jack muttered, making us laugh even harder. "Right. What's the latest with my sister and her asshole stalker? You said something about a new plan."

"There was an incident yesterday with a letter from him," I explained. "It's clear he's getting angry and escalating, so we're going to use that to our advantage and try to catch him so we can finish this."

"Legally," Archer interjected. "With cops and restraining orders and such," Archer interrupted.

I rolled my eyes, and so did Vince. Clearly, we were open to other, *non-legal* options that Archer may not be.

We filled him in about the letter and how she was holding up, plus all the latest information we had on him, before we laid out the plan.

"We're moving her car back to the parking lot tomorrow, with the tracker in the original spot, and position the car right in front of the pub so it's visible," Vince said. "The hope is Rupnik tracks the car and takes notice, and we'll be ready."

"Tomorrow night?" Jack asked, seemingly shocked it was so soon. "Guys, can we hold off till the end of the week instead?"

"The pub is slowest on Tuesdays, so we'll be dealing with the fewest number of people nearby," I clarified.

"Look, I'm not asking we wait weeks. I'd just like to actually be in my own apartment a few days and not be completely jet-lagged for this," Jack argued.

"Jack," Archer cut in. "While I'm pretty sure the letter itself was delivered from a local homeless guy, Rupnik's obviously in town and saw her to know she was working last night," Archer explained to him. "We don't want to give him too much time to think or plan anything out. I got a guy I know on the force here. He and his partner are gonna come have dinner in plain clothes at the pub tomorrow on us, so we also have a police presence in case he shows and makes a scene."

"Ellie works at night, but after we get the new guys onboarded and finish up a client call tomorrow afternoon, we'll go down there and eat dinner and hang out at the pub until she is off for the night to have a presence in case he comes early," Archer detailed.

"I'm also going to help out at the bar with her and Tammy so she's got protection close by," I conveyed to Jack since I knew he was going to be concerned about that.

"When she's done with her shift, we'll get her back upstairs and put her in Wade's apartment for the night," Vince said and looked at me with a bit of warning to let me know Jack was not going to like this.

"Why the hell would she stay with Wade?" Jack asked. "I'll be back and likely able to meet you all for dinner or shortly thereafter unless traffic makes Vince and I late. She can keep staying in my apartment, and I'll watch her."

Vince's gaze shifted to me, and I knew it had more to do with the fact that he knew I was sleeping with Ellie and hadn't told Jack, but before I could say anything to Jack, Archer broke in.

"Jack, it's Archer. Hear me out on this." Archer leaned closer to the phone and started to explain. "I'm working on getting it fixed, but right now, your apartment is registered in your full name. It won't take this guy much effort at all if he searches, or pays someone to search for him, to find out you live above the building. It's going to be safer for her to stay close to you, but not that close."

I calmed a little, knowing Archer made a great point that I hadn't thought of because I was just being selfish in my reasoning. I did want her staying with me for her safety, but I also wanted her with me tonight because I needed to finally tell her that I wanted to make her mine.

"Ugh. Alright," Jack conceded, begrudgingly.

We wrapped up our conversation with some more info about the two new hires, and Vince got Jack's flight info so he could pick him up from the airport tomorrow.

Ellie was off today and was trying to clean up Jack's apartment before he got back. I texted her to tell her I was taking her out to dinner tonight. I needed to have a conversation with her about us, but I also realized that if I wanted her to believe that I was ready to actually try doing the relationship thing, that I needed to treat it like that. That meant I needed to take her out on real dates and woo and charm her like real boyfriends did.

I finished up my work and headed upstairs to get ready. I'd made reservations on the early side because I wanted to be able to come back here and watch a movie with her at my place. It had become kind of our routine when neither of us worked late, and I found I enjoyed it.

I walked across the hall and knocked on Jack's door. Yeah, I had a key, but again, I was trying to be all chivalrous and stuff, so I decided to knock instead.

She opened the door wearing a blue dress that wasn't fancy, but it suited her and matched her eyes perfectly. The neckline cut down in the front, just enough to show me a little tease of cleavage, but I knew what those perfect breasts of hers looked like, and I found myself fighting getting hard just looking at her.

I needed to focus. Boyfriend mode. What would a good boyfriend do?

"You look very nice, Ellie," I told her as I resisted the urge to pick her up and take her right there on the floor next to her kitchen.

"Thanks." She smiled at me. "You look pretty nice yourself." She looked me up and down, interest clearly written on her face, making it even harder for me to control my dick.

"You ready?" I asked her, realizing it was better to leave the apartment so I wasn't tempted.

She grabbed her purse, and we made our way down to my car. Knowing that asshole could still be around, I made sure to give my surroundings an extra glance just in case but saw nothing out of the ordinary.

Conversation in the car and at the restaurant was light but good. We enjoyed each other's company, and I realized that having a woman who was beautiful, kind, easy to talk to, and who you enjoyed spending time with was not an easy find. Women like that were not a dime a dozen, making me realize even more how lucky I was to have found her.

"Not that I'm complaining..." Ellie pushed her empty plate away from her. "But why did you want to go out to a nice restaurant tonight?" she asked me with genuine interest in her eyes.

I realized I didn't really explain my motives in my text and might need to spell it out more. I might as well just lay all my cards on the table so she didn't think this was just about me getting laid.

"I don't want you to think I'm only interested in you for sex, Ellie," I told her. "I'm attracted to you, but I also care for you and enjoy spending time with you. I figured it was about time to take you out on a proper date."

She smiled at me, and her cheeks turned pink. I realized I'd either embarrassed her or she was nervous. Maybe this wasn't the best location to have this chat.

"You want dessert or to just go back and watch a movie at my place?" I asked, hoping she picked the latter so I could talk to her in a more private setting.

"Are you trying to get me to Netflix and chill with you," she teased, smirking at me. "Just so you know, I usually have a very strict policy of no sex on a first date."

Her cheeks got a little pinker, and my dick hardened just at the mention of sex out of her mouth.

"Good to know," I informed her and then grinned and flagged the waitress for our check.

She grabbed her purse, and I held her hand as I walked her to the car. As I opened her door, I gently grabbed her arm to turn her toward me. I kissed her hard but quick then slid my mouth across her cheek before whispering in her ear.

"Think I may be able to convince you to make an exception on your first date rule?" I asked her as my hand on her arm slid to her waist and pulled her flush against me. I kissed her harder now before sliding my tongue over her lips, seeking entry, and she opened for me, allowing me to taste her.

"I've been wanting to do that all night," I told her as I let go and helped her into the car.

I took a moment to readjust myself as I walked around to the driver's seat. Focus, I told myself. *Conversation first. Then, hopefully she is on board with your plan, and you can have sex.*

If only one head would listen to the other.

I could sense Wade was being vigilant as we walked back into the apartment. His hand was holding mine, and he kept me close. I didn't mind.

Tonight was an enigma for me. Wade's random text earlier today telling me we were going out to dinner and to dress nice threw me off. First, as a woman, the term "nice" did not tell you much. Did that mean jeans and a cute top with heels? A dress with glam hair and makeup and lots of jewelry? I tried to prod the name of the restaurant out of him so I could look into what kind of place we were going to, but all I got in response was, "It's a surprise...be ready at 5:30." Men. Why did men never understand the importance of a heads-up and details? Women needed to know where we were going, mostly so we knew what to wear, and we needed advance notice of this so we had enough time to get ready.

I had spent most of the day cleaning up Jack's apart-

ment, getting stuff ready for when he came home tomorrow. Also, getting caught up on laundry and school stuff,
so when his text came through, my mind started freaking
out with what to wear and why Wade wanted to go out to
someplace "nice" in the first place.

Dinner was great though. He'd looked so good when
he showed up to pick me up in his dark jeans and a navy
dress shirt with the sleeves rolled up to just below his
elbows.

I was glad at that moment I'd picked this dress. It was
a cornflower blue color, sleeveless, and went down to
about two inches above my knees. It was relatively plain,
but it had a V-neck, and it dipped low enough to show off
a hint of cleavage, which he clearly noticed when he
picked me up.

I had my hair in loose waves, which I'd noticed he
liked because he often ran his hands through them while
we watched a movie. I'd also worn sandals with a small
heel. I didn't usually wear heels because I was already tall,
but Wade was several inches taller than me and I felt sexy
wearing them, so I'd put them on. He clearly liked them
too, because when we got back into his apartment, I set
my purse on the table and then walked over to the edge of
the couch to take the shoes off, when he came up in front
of me and told me to keep them on.

"Is this where you try to seduce me into having your
way with me on a first date?" I teased him, putting my
palms on his chest and smiling up at him.

"Woman, do not tempt me right now," he said, looking

serious, but his eyes were definitely full of lust. "Those sexy-as-hell shoes you have on right now are working my control, and I'd like to talk with you first."

I didn't know why I decided to play with fire when it came to him, but he looked so lost right now, I wanted to guide him back to the fun-loving Wade from earlier.

"What would you like to talk about?" I asked as I moved one palm down the front of his shirt to latch on to his belt buckle, the other hand to the bulge in his pants.

He moved quickly and grabbed hold of my wrists and kept them in place.

"I'm not going to pretend last night wasn't amazing, and that I wouldn't love a repeat right now," Wade said with a small smile. "But I'm also not going to pretend I don't want you around for other reasons too. I care about you Ellie and not just because you're Jack's sister."

What did he just say?

"Commitment scares me—not because I don't want to be with someone, but because I'm afraid of what being with someone, especially while sleeping, would do. But now I've realized that I'm more scared of losing something important. And I don't want to lose you."

"What are you saying?" I asked, looking him in the eyes, and I saw the hope in his.

"I'm saying I want to try this with you, to give us a chance," Wade said in return. "I want to see where it goes."

"Are you sure you're not just saying this because the

sex is good?" I smirked, hoping he couldn't see through my nervous attempt at teasing him.

"I didn't think I was a good-enough man capable of a relationship, but you make me want to be that man, Ellie," Wade said, his voice strong, but I could feel the nervous energy coming off him. "I'm not saying I won't screw up, but I promise I will never hurt you on purpose."

"Wade, you are absolutely a good man. Why would you ever doubt that?" I told him, cupping his face so he understood that I never thought he was anything but a good man.

"Ellie," he said, and I knew he was thinking about his night terrors and the possibility of hurting me, even if it was accidental.

I'd spent enough time second-guessing this thing building between us. But why? Was it Randall? Because that wasn't fair to Wade since they were nothing alike and he had proven time and time again that they weren't even a remotely close comparison. He might think he wasn't ready for a relationship, yet he was the one willing to take the risk, even though he doubted himself. I could take that risk with him and be the one to show him—show him that a relationship doesn't need to be perfect, that he didn't need to be perfect, for there to be something between us.

"I know I don't deserve you, but I'm a selfish bastard, and I don't want to let you go," he said, shaking me out of my private thoughts. "I know this might seem like a big shift, but I've thought about it a lot, and I know what I want."

I smiled at him and took a deep breath.

"I'm in," I told him, my smile now bigger as I leaned in and gave him a small kiss.

He moved his hands to my wrists, effectively keeping them in place on the sides of his face as he continued to kiss me.

Things got heated, but not in the fast-paced way I was used to. His kiss was more like he was cherishing the moment and wanting it to last. He tilted my head and deepened the kiss, and I felt the world spin around me. We were standing side by side next to the couch, and then he grabbed behind my thighs and lifted my legs to wrap around his hips. He turned and started walking us back to the bedroom, all while still kissing me senseless.

He lowered my legs to the ground next to the edge of the bed. He moved his hands to my back and slowly unzipped my dress, as he stared deep into my eyes. There were so many emotions swirling in his eyes right now, from lust to happiness to surprise.

His hands moved to my shoulders and slid the dress off my arms until it fell to the ground. I heard a small growl as he saw the pale blue and black lace bra and matching panties I was wearing.

"God, Ellie, you make it really hard to take this slow," he said, his voice straining like he was about to snap.

"I didn't ask you to take it slow," I whispered to him.

"Ellie, back in there," he used his thumb to point back

toward the living room. "You agreed to try this with me. Take the chance on us. What you didn't realize was that makes you mine. Mine to protect, mine to take care of. *Mine*," he said as he stroked his hands down the front of my body.

I felt chills all through my body at the adoration in his voice.

"I'm also not good with words to explain to you how I feel, but I can show you," he said, breathing heavily. "So, I want to do this right and take it slow so I can show you how much you mean to me, but I need to hold back to do that."

"I don't want you to hold back, Wade," I told him as I moved to start to unbutton his dress shirt, realizing he was struggling with the war in his mind. "Give me you. The *real* you. *All of you*."

He moaned but didn't move as I continued to undress him. We were both standing there in just our underwear, staring at each other.

He was looking at me reverently, as though I was the best thing he had ever seen and he couldn't get enough of it. I had never felt more vulnerable but also treasured in my life.

Clearly, he'd had enough looking and needed more touching, because the next thing I knew, he lifted me and dropped me on the bed on my back, and then he was on top of me.

His kisses were hard and urgent, but his hands were moving so slowly over my body, as though they were worshipping it. He reached around my back and unclasped my bra. Then he took his mouth off mine momentarily to lean back and remove the lace and drop it to the floor beside the bed.

He began gently stroking all over my chest before stopping right over my heart. I was sure he could feel the thumping beat underneath his hand, as my heart was beating rapidly as my chest rose and fell with my heavy breaths.

"You are so incredibly beautiful, Ellie," he said to me quietly as he looked all over my body, admiring it.

"Show me," I said quietly.

His mouth was on me a moment later, and my body was spinning again. Not because he was moving me, but because his kiss was making me dizzy. He slid my under-wear off, and his hand was right back there delicately rubbing between my thighs, building a burn that I knew would be intense. He slid his hand over my mound and pushed gently down on my clit with his thumb, and my mind went blank. I moaned loudly, and he pulled away from my mouth. I could feel his breath on me, but his eyes were on mine. His hand was still moving, and I felt his fingers enter me as his thumb still worked the bundle of nerves near the entrance. My back arched involuntar-ily, and my head rolled back as a sound I had never made before left me. It was a cross between a moan and a whimper.

He took advantage of my chest being in his face and latched on to my nipple with his mouth, drawing hard. I felt that twinge from my head to my toes, and it felt amazing. The pressure built between my legs, and I knew my orgasm was about to burst. I wanted him to be inside me when it happened, but I also couldn't speak. I could barely move.

His fingers curled inside me and his thumb pressed harder on the nub and swirled. My orgasm crashed over me, and I saw stars. The pleasure in my voice was mixed with my moans. I felt him moving around, but I couldn't open my eyes yet. I couldn't move anything. My limbs had stopped working.

"Ellie, look at me," I heard Wade say, but I couldn't focus right now. "Ellie, sweetheart, look at me."

I slowly opened my eyes and looked into his. He lifted my body and scooted me back further onto the bed. His body was now hovering over me, and he was looking at me with lust and pure bliss on his face, mixed with a little smirk.

I mustered a small smile in return.

His right hand cupped my face, his thumb stroking my cheek. He used his left arm to support his body on the mattress. Then he removed his right hand from my face and used it to slide his cock to my entrance. He swirled it around my now very wet entrance, and I let out a small moan again and closed my eyes.

"Eyes open, Ellie," he said, commanding me.

It was a struggle, but I got them open just in time for him to slide into me, and it felt incredible. I'd never had a guy inside me bare, so I didn't know if it normally felt this good, but this was miles above anything I'd ever experienced.

"Ellie, you feel so good," he groaned. "Never felt this good. Ever."

"Don't hold back, Wade," I told him softly. "Make love to me."

His mouth was on mine again, and he was kissing me with everything he had. I struggled to breathe as he moved in and out of me slowly but firmly. I'd just orgasmed, but I could feel another one building inside me. It felt different though.

"God, Ellie," he said as he tore his mouth off mine but kept his lips only a breath away from mine, and I knew he felt it too.

"Come, baby. Give it to me," he said. "I'm not going to make it much longer."

He reached down and rubbed my hyper-sensitive clit, and that did it. One caress, and I was floating. I felt like my body was lifted into the air, and then I felt nothing but pure bliss. I cried out and heard him groan deeply as he slammed into me, gripping my hip with his hand. Feeling his release inside me while I was still coming down from my orgasm was such a weird feeling, but I loved it.

He collapsed on top of me, and while it made it hard to breathe, I loved feeling his weight there. He was peppering my face and neck with small, light kisses.

"I'm so lucky to have you," Wade said quietly, and my heart swelled.

I really wanted to respond back that I loved him, but I

knew it was too soon. It took everything from him to ask me to take the next step. I didn't want to spook him by sharing with him that I loved him. Not yet.

Several minutes later, he got up and walked to the bathroom, coming back with a warm washcloth. He leaned down to kiss me as he cleaned me up. When he once again left the bed, I still couldn't feel my legs, so I stayed there, unmoving.

He came back moments later with some water and settled beside me. I fell asleep moments later, wrapped in his arms, and realized I had never felt more content in my life.

20

ELLIE

I woke earlier this morning with a huge smile on my face. Cocooned in Wade's arms while he peppered my shoulder and neck with kisses that eventually led to other glorious things was a perfect way to start my day. I thought back to the talk we'd had last night where he told me I was it for him and we were going to give this a shot.

I didn't think I was a good-enough man capable of a relationship, but you make me want to be that man, Ellie. I'm not saying I won't screw up, but I promise I will never hurt you on purpose.

Wade was so complex but also kind, protective, encouraging, supportive, and it didn't hurt that he was too handsome for his own good. I was ready. Ready to move on from Randall and take these next steps with Wade.

The other great part was that my brother was back in the States and finally coming back to Georgia tonight.

Which reminded me of my conversation with Wade this morning.

"This morning, move your stuff in here," Wade told me.

"Like move into your apartment?" I asked him, kind of shocked because this seemed fast.

"Babe," he said calmly as he stroked my hair while lying next to me in bed. "I want you in my bed. Plus, your brother comes home today, and he's gonna want his bed back. You think it's too fast or you want something closer to school, then I'll help you look for your own apartment, but you're either gonna be sleepin' here in my bed, or I'll be in yours every night, so short-term, just move your stuff in here."

What he said made sense, but it still seemed fast to me. At the same time, the thought of sharing a space with him didn't scare me like it had with Randall. Plus, I didn't really want to share a space with my brother. That had only been my temporary solution when I originally moved here.

Jack and I had been texting back and forth the last few days, and I knew he'd talked with Wade and Vince yesterday about the plan with my car. Apparently, Jack wasn't happy about the timing of the plan, nor was he happy about me staying in Wade's apartment. I agreed with the guys and had told my brother as much via text.

I hadn't had a chance to really talk to Jack about where Wade and I stood yet, because I wanted that to be in person where he wasn't distracted. Hopefully I could explain to him tonight at dinner so he understood, and we would stick with the original plan of me staying with Wade tonight.

After Wade worshipped my body this morning, we went for a walk together down by the river on one of the trails—something we had done several times now and I really enjoyed. Especially when Mr. Alpha Macho Man held my hand the entire time we walked.

When we returned, he went to the gym, and I stayed behind to clean up before my shift so I could get Jack's place back in order before he arrived.

Wade came back into the apartment as I was filling out some forms online for school registration.

"You excited about school?" he asked as he walked up behind me, moved my hair off my shoulder, and leaned down to kiss my neck.

Heat moved through my body instantly, and I breathed out a sound of contentment.

"Yeah, it feels like a long time coming, so I'm happy I finally get to do it," I told him, sighing as I thought of how proud Gran would be of me. I wish she were here. Not only would she be happy about school, but she would really like Wade for me.

"Let me shower, and then I need to grab a few things at the office before we head to the pub, okay?" he asked.

"Yeah, I'll be done with these forms in just a few minutes, and then I'll get ready," I told him.

I watched as he walked toward the bedroom, and I thought how lucky I was that he was mine.

Wade and I walked into the pub together with him holding my hand. We got to the bar area where Sam and Tammy were working. Beth was also by the bar, closing out her tabs because she was coming off shift soon. When I said hi to her, she looked at us and her eyes moved directly to my hand entwined with Wade's. Her eyes went wide, but then she looked at me with a weird smile on her face.

"Good to see you. Have a fun shift," she said before walking away. I knew she'd suspected there was something going on between us, and I'd told her there couldn't be, so maybe she realized things had changed.

I let go of Wade's hand and went to the back-office space to put my purse down and say hi to Chuck before walking back out to the front. Wade was talking to Tammy when I came out, and I assumed it was to discuss the plan for the next day and to keep an eye out. He turned to me when I walked out and gave me a small smile. He took the few small steps toward me, put his hand around the side of my neck, and gave me a quick kiss on my forehead right in front of Tammy and everyone at the bar, and then left, saying he would be back soon. I stood there silently with my fingers barely touching my lips, looking at nowhere in particular.

"Looks like *one* of you isn't afraid to rush things," Tammy said with a small chuckle and knowing smile.

She knew my hesitation with moving too quickly with

Wade, but I hadn't filled her in since Wade and I talked yesterday. Once we slowed down a bit, I would give her the latest details because I could certainly use her sage advice to help me work through my nerves.

My mind kept going back to the conversation with Wade last night. I could sense he was still holding back a little, unsure of his own worth, but that made me more determined to also put myself out there. I was ready to move forward, to take that leap. I wanted to break those walls down to show him that he deserved a good partner by his side, just like I did. He was worth it, and so was I. With that thought, I tried to get my focus back to work, knowing I would tell him tonight how I felt.

It wasn't too busy yet, but the dinner rush would be coming soon so Tammy and I spent the next thirty minutes trying to get everything prepped for when we filled up.

"Hey, Ellie," I heard Beth call to me. "The boss wants to see you back in his office." She leaned into me and spoke in a quieter tone. "You might want to go quick, cause he seems upset."

I wondered if something with Randall had come up. I nodded to Tammy, who'd heard and told me she would take care of the guys at the end of the bar for me. As I set my drying towel down to head to the back office, Beth added one more thing.

"He went to take the trash out really quick, but you can either wait in his office or meet him by the back door when he comes in if that's easier. I'm done for the day, so

I'll follow you out. Bye Tammy!" she said as she waved bye to Tammy and followed me through the door to the kitchen and toward the back of the building.

I glanced in his office, but he wasn't there, which meant he must still be outside.

After the mystery letter the other night, Wade and the guys had told me not to go outside alone, and I wasn't stupid. I would go out with Beth and just stand by the back door as he walked back from the dumpster. Plus, technically if he was already out there, I wouldn't be alone, and if he really was in a bad mood because of Randall, I wanted to know what was going on.

Beth opened the back door for me, and I followed her out. Our dumpster wasn't far from the back door, maybe forty to fifty feet at most, so I could see it as soon as I opened the door. There was a light above the back door, and it was very bright—for security reasons—but even with the extra light, I didn't see Wade. Just as I was about to call out to him, something flashed on my left side just around the door, and something hard hit my head. It hurt so bad, and I felt myself lurch forward, and then everything went black.

21

WADE

This meeting was taking longer than I had planned, but it would all be worth it in the end. In the other room, our two newest hires, Dane Enderson and Axel Skarsgård—the two guys my sister had recommended—were finally done with all their onboarding and were being shown around the building by Ruthie. Archer and I were going over our final plans for Operation Douche Canoe, as we had aptly named it, to deal with Ellie's ex. Vince had just walked in, letting us know he had moved Ellie's car back to the front of the pub—exactly where we wanted it—front and center for her ex to see. Happy that everything seemed to be in place, I leaned back in my chair opposite Archer at his desk, with Vince next to me in the other chair. He was about to leave to go get Jack from the airport and bring him back so we could all have dinner downstairs at the pub.

In my hand from when I pulled up my text thread

earlier from Jack to say he was boarding his flight to Atlanta, my phone vibrated with a call. I looked down to see it was Tammy and knew she wouldn't call unless it was important since she knew I was up here with the guys, finishing this meeting up.

I answered the phone deciding to get straight to the point. "What's wrong?"

"You still in your meeting?" she asked, but I could sense the seriousness in her tone.

"Just ending it. Why?" I asked as I heard her moving around.

"Pull up the cameras to the back exit of the pub, and do it now," she said frantically.

"What's going on, Tammy?" I asked firmly as I put the phone on speaker, set it on the desk, and leaned over and grabbed the computer mouse from the desk. I swiveled the desktop monitor so I could see it. I was frantically switching over to our screen that let us see all the cameras in the building while Tammy talked.

"Beth came up here and told Ellie you needed to see her right away but that you were taking the trash out and she would follow her to the back door to wait for you, but I knew you were supposedly in your meeting, not to mention Sam just took the trash out right before he left his shift," she said fast, hardly taking a breath. "It took me a second to remember that, and when I came back here, I...I can't find either of them. She's gone, Wade. I can't find Ellie," she said calmly but with noticeable fear in her voice.

I felt my stomach drop. Archer took the mouse from me as he looked up at me.

"Go. I'll check the cameras and call you. Go!" he told me as I pushed back my chair and practically sprinted out of the office door to get downstairs. Phone in my hand, I kept talking to Tammy, trying to understand what happened.

"It might be Beth," she said.

Beth may have had a role in this. It made sense because she worked with Ellie, so she would have had proximity to get to her, but why?

"I can't find Beth, but she was also done with her shift, so she may have left and not seen anything," Tammy tried to say, but I knew the other words she was thinking too. "But why would she have told her that you were waiting for her when you had a meeting? This isn't adding up."

"No, it doesn't. I'm on my way down there," I told her and hung up as I raced as fast as I could down the stairs.

I passed the front office and yelled to Ruthie to get upstairs and help Archer and Vince immediately. We needed all the help we could get. I exited the front door and ran around the building to the back entrance, where Tammy was currently standing in the doorway, looking in every direction.

"Talk to me," I said firmly.

"You dropped Ellie off to start her shift. We were restocking everything and getting ready for the dinner rush, and Beth came by as she was leaving for the night," Tammy started in. "Beth said that you told her you needed to see Ellie right away, and then as she was walking back there, she mentioned you were just taking the trash out so Ellie should wait for you by the door. She said she would walk out there with her, so I didn't worry initially because I knew she wouldn't be alone. I'm an idiot. I'm sorry, Wade."

Knowing she felt terrible, I shook my head, trying to reassure her.

"Beth has worked here for over a year. It's normal to trust her. Don't beat yourself up Tammy. We'll find her," I told her, hoping if I said it out loud, it would come true. My phone rang in my pocket, and when I saw it was Archer, I hoped he had good news.

"What," I snapped without an introduction.

"He grabbed her," he said in my ear, and I felt the anger rising in me and it became harder to breathe. "He was waiting right outside the door and hit her on the back of the head with something as soon as she walked out."

"Where the hell was Beth?" I asked, wondering why she didn't scream or run back inside to get Tammy or Chuck.

"All evidence is pointing to her helping the dude," he said angrily, but he also sensed my anger rising, so he continued to talk. "She helped him secure her and then left the parking lot swiftly in her car. I sent Dane and Axel over to her place right now to track her down and get answers. I called the cops. They're on their way here to the office. Ruthie and Diego are going to stay here and walk them through what happened while we go get her."

"We don't know where he took her, though. He could be on his way to Tennessee or Florida for all we know!" I practically yelled into the phone.

"Wade, calm down for just a second and let me explain," he said in his authoritative, yet surprisingly very calm voice. "She has a tracking device on her, and Vince just pulled it up now. It's moving, so we're going to follow it."

"No, her phone is still at the bar. She doesn't have that with her," I told him.

"No, Ruthie gave her one, and it's working," he said.

While part of me was relieved that we knew where she was. I was also livid that he'd kept this from me.

"Ruthie put a tracker on her? Why the hell didn't you tell me?" I yelled.

"It's not what you think. I'll explain in the car," he said suddenly from right behind me. He and Vince were there, apparently having run down through the building and out back to come get me. "Vince has the tracker pulled up. Let's go," he said urgently and started jogging to the SUV in the side parking lot.

I turned to Tammy and instructed her to call Sam and see if he could come back for a bit so she could go help Ruthie with the cops when they arrived. She nodded, and I ran off to the vehicle.

Vince was in the driver's seat and starting the car when I hopped in the back. Archer, who was in the front passenger seat, was already talking to me before I could get my question out.

"Ruthie wears a necklace with pink boxing gloves on it," he said, and I tried to think back to whether I'd seen her wear it before while he continued. "I gave that to her. It has a tracking device built into it in case something ever happened."

There was a lot to unpack with that statement, and I wanted to ask him more, but right now I needed to focus on finding Ellie.

"She mentioned Ellie commenting on it a while back, and since we all knew Ellie was having issues with her ex, she wanted to know if we could give one to Ellie as well," Archer explained. "I thought it was a good idea, so Ruthie picked out a yellow pair of gloves for Ellie that attached to her necklace, and I added the tracking device to it. Ruthie only gave it to her a few days ago."

I recalled seeing it on her this morning as I was exploring her body when we woke up but didn't ask about it because my mind was consumed with other thoughts.

Her beautiful face popped into my mind, and all I could think of was that I'd finally made the decision to take a chance with her, and now I may not get it. We needed to find her. I *had* to find her.

I just hoped we could find her in time before that asshole hurt her—or worse.

22

ELLIE

God, my head hurt so bad. My eyes opened slowly, but I wanted to close them right back because the light made my head hurt worse. I realized, though, in the brief moment my eyes were open, that I didn't recognize the space. I tried to open them again, succeeding enough to take in the fact that I definitely did not know where I was.

Even though it hurt using my brain, things started to come back to me. At the pub, looking for Wade. Beth walking out the back door with me, only to be hit by something. And then nothing. This looked like a house, but I didn't think I'd ever been here before.

I realized I was on a bed, but when I went to move my arms to sit up, I couldn't. I looked up and realized my arms were tied to the top of the bed. Okay this wasn't good. I started to pull my arms hard to try to release them, but there was no give. I could feel the panic rising in me, because, let's face it, no one hit you over the head, took you to a strange house, and tied you up for a good reason.

My legs weren't tied, so I tried to scoot myself into more of a sitting position closer to the headboard. There was a window to my right and a big tree outside, so I couldn't see whether I was in a neighborhood, on a farm, or anything. Just then, I heard the door open and a familiar voice that brought chills to my spine.

"Glad to see you finally woke up, Elliana," Randall said from the doorway with a big smile on his face and a glass of what looked like water in his hand. "You've been very bad, Elliana, and now we have to talk."

Fear filled my body, because I knew that look on his face. It was the one he would get when he was mad and about to get violent with me.

"I'm very displeased you tried to run away from me, Elliana," he said appearing calm on the outside, but I knew he wasn't. "But what really distresses me is that you have been unfaithful."

Oh God. Wade. Is that why I couldn't find Wade outside? Did he hurt him too? And what happened to Beth?

"Wh... Where's Beth?" I asked as my voice cracked a little. "Did you hurt her?"

"Hurt Beth?" He chuckled a little. "Of course not. She's been helping me all along on this little recovery mission."

That answer shocked me, and he must have seen it on

my face because his smile grew bigger as he walked further into the room. I tried to curl my body up more, but my hands being tied above me made that much harder.

"That first time you answered the phone at the pub, I was already here in Georgia," he started to explain with a smirk on his face that exuded hostility. "I tracked your car here, but what I didn't know was whether you were parked here for the pub or something nearby. When you answered the phone, I knew I'd hit the jackpot. Right after you hung up, Beth walked out of the pub. I simply explained to her that I was your boyfriend and that we'd had a small spat but I was planning to get you back. She was more than happy to give me your schedule so that I could surprise you."

The way he said surprise told me he didn't mean it in a good way, but Beth likely took it that way.

"I have to admit that I thought he was a bit creepy at first and wasn't sure I was going to help him," Beth said, stepping into the door frame behind Randall with a small grin on her face, which quickly morphed into something downright evil. "But then you had to go and steal something that wasn't yours. Wade is mine! He and I were getting close and were going to be lovers if you hadn't stepped in," she said as she started walking towards me.

It all started coming back to me. How she kept asking about whether Wade and I were a thing.

"Oh God," I gasped. "*You* wrote the note with the tip money," I surmised out loud.

"Not just that," she said, pride written across her face. "All the things to your car? That was me." She giggled a little maniacally. "I could tell they drove you crazy."

This was not the same Beth I knew. The woman in front of me was unhinged.

I shook my head, saying, "I didn't do anything to you. Why—"

"You lied to me!" she screamed, her voice rising. "You told me and Tammy you weren't interested in men, that you were giving up dating—but you lied! You were with him the whole time. He held your hand, he kissed you. I saw it with my own two eyes, and I knew you had put your whore hands all over him and slept with him!"

Her voice had risen to a full-blown yell. "The only way he would betray me like that is if you tricked him—if you seduced him away from me!"

"Calm down, Beth," Randall interrupted for the first time since she started going off the rails, his voice edged with irritation, as if even he found her sudden outburst exhausting. "I can assure you she will be punished for cheating on me."

Then he turned back to me, his eyes filled with venom —and a twisted excitement, no doubt from the things he planned to do to me.

Oddly, Randall's words seem to have an effect on her. She calmed down instantly.

"Yes, I need to leave anyway, because when Wade finds out that you left him to go back to Randall, he will be very upset, and I plan to help soothe him and return us to the wonderful relationship we had before you arrived," she said, nodding to herself as though her crazy thoughts would actually turn into reality.

"Go ahead, Beth. I have everything I need here. Your services are no longer needed. I'll walk you out," he said and followed her out the door.

I realized I didn't have much time, but I had to figure out a way out of here, because when he came back, he would likely beat me to within inches of my life, if he even let me live at all. I turned my body to see how my arms were tied to the bed to see if I could position myself to loosen them or get out. I struggled and was able to get my mouth close to try to use my teeth to undo the knots, but they were on tight.

Bang! Bang!

I flinched at the sound of the gunshots. Two, and not far. I froze. Who was that? Why were there no screams? I tried to work even more frantically at my ties because I had no idea what was happening in the other part of the house, but I knew I couldn't stay there.

"Ah, Elliana, nice try, but you will not be leaving." Randall came back into the room with a gun in his hand as he wiped it on his shirt. "Sorry about the delay, but as helpful as Beth has been up to this point, I don't like loose ends, and sadly, she became someone who knew a little too much."

I realized now that the gunshots came from Randall, and he must have shot her.

"Y-You... you killed her?" I stuttered, asking what I

already knew was likely true but still needing the confirmation.

"It pains me a little because she was so helpful—especially when that boss of yours started to encroach on what belonged to me," he said, his voice laced with even more malice. "But I also couldn't have her running back to that man and telling him what she knows. However, I understand she helped us, and I know this upsets you, so we can take her with us, and I will bury her with the others."

"Others?" I squeaked, and his face oddly softened.

"Sweetheart, we aren't the only ones who know this relationship was meant to be. But there have been a few bumps along the way, so I've had to remove a few obstacles."

I had been scared before, but now I was terrified—not just at the fact that he had obviously killed other people, but at how easily he spoke about it, as if burying them was just another chore.

I thought of Katie. I knew she would never willingly help Randall, knowing the monster he had become, but she had been radio silent for the last few days. I was worried about her.

"Katie?" I asked with a bit of a cry.

"That bitch?" he snarled, and his demeanor changed once again. "No, but I should have killed her with your grandma for trying to interfere in our connection."

My heart stopped. Gran. My beautiful, sweet Gran.

"Gran," I whispered with a huge lump in my throat.

"She fell down the stairs...I found her when I got home from work."

"Of course she did, sweetheart." He nodded and moved his hand to my leg as he sat on the bed next to me. I scooted my leg away as best I could, but he grabbed ahold of my ankle tight and squeezed.

"She didn't want you moving in with me, and she wanted you to go away to college." He started shaking his head in disbelief. "She was preventing us from taking the next step, and I couldn't let that happen. You didn't need to go to college. I could have given us everything we needed. She just wouldn't let that happen."

I stared at him in disbelief.

"I went to your house to have a chat with her and explain you would be moving in with me and that was final, and she had the nerve to tell me no." He shook his head, as if he couldn't believe someone would tell him anything other than what he wanted to hear.

"She was old. Old people fall down the stairs all the time. I just simply assisted her," he said with a shrug.

I was overwhelmed with emotions—anger that he killed her, sadness for my poor grandma who had done nothing wrong, and fear because I now realized he had no problem killing. If he was so flippant about their deaths, what would stop him from killing me too?

I thought of my brother and how I would never get to see him again. Wade...Sweet, handsome Wade. He finally opened himself up to being with someone, and he picked me. If I didn't make it out of this, he would go right back to his hidey hole, and I couldn't let him do that. I needed to survive so I could heal with him. The two of us together.

Randall must have misinterpreted the look on my face, because his softened a bit as he looked at me.

"It's okay now, darling. There is no one else in our way," he said, staring at me and obviously very happy with himself. "You will, of course, need to be punished because this long scavenger hunt you've sent me on has gotten me in trouble with work, and we cannot have that. But we're destined to be together, so we'll get through this and come out better on the other side," he said, putting his hand on my cheek.

I flinched and he smiled.

I knew in that moment I had to get out of there. I had to find some way of distracting him and finding a way out.

"O-Okay, Randall," I said, trying to placate him to buy myself some time. "I understand. I have to use the restroom. Can you help me, honey?" I hoped the endearment and submission would allow me to get out of these restraints.

"Nice try, Elliana." He moved the hand from my cheek to my neck and squeezed. "You aren't leaving this bed until you've been punished, and you will be punished thoroughly." His smug smile came back onto his face. "And you can scream as loud as you want, and no one will hear you. I rented this house for the week because it's remote with no neighbors anywhere nearby. Exactly what we needed for your punishment. Then we'll head home to Tennessee where we belong."

He stood up from the bed and started to take the belt off his pants. I began to shake, knowing what was about to happen. He walked over to me, and I started to scramble up on the bed. I couldn't use my arms, but I could use my legs, so when he got close, I kicked my right leg out and got him right in the crotch. He screamed in pain and fell to his knees. He was heaving with one hand on the floor and the other over his family jewels.

"You will pay for that, Elliana," he growled at me with a tinge of pain in his voice.

I was frantically trying to think of how to get out of this situation. *Think, Ellie. Think!*

Still cupping his junk with one hand and breathing heavily, he sat up a little and used his other hand to grab my leg and pull himself up. Once upright, he sat on me so I couldn't move. His weight on my legs prevented me from kicking out. I started to scream, even though I knew it was unlikely anyone could hear me. I only got a brief scream out, and then his free hand was on my neck.

"You'll be sorry you did that, Elliana," he wheezed, but with the full force of anger.

He squeezed my throat harder, and it began getting hard to breathe. I tried moving but I couldn't do much with my arms still tethered to the headboard and his body pinning my legs. I was frantic, trying anything as I felt my chest tighten, struggling to get a breath. I closed my eyes, trying to focus, when all of a sudden, the restricting feeling on my throat was gone and I heard Randall yell. I opened my eyes as I gasped in a huge breath. I saw Randall being thrown to the ground by a man in black, and the next thing I knew, I saw Wade's beautiful face in front of me. I wondered if I'd blacked out. Yes, I must have blacked out, and Wade was now the angel of death taking me away.

23

WADE

We followed Ellie's dot all the way out of town—a good twenty-minute drive under normal circumstances—but it was rush hour, so traffic was bad, doubling our travel time. Her dot had been stopped for at least ten minutes, and I was panicked. I tried to draw on my Army training to stay focused and calm, but I was struggling.

Vince's phone rang, and he answered it through the car speaker.

"What have you got?" he asked, straight to the point.

"We're here at Beth's place," Axel explained quickly. "She's not here. Car isn't here, and we got in the apartment and she's not inside either. Do you want us to go look somewhere else for her?"

"No, just go back to the office and help Tammy and Ruthie with the police. Thanks, man," Vince said as he ended the call.

"Where the fuck did she go?" I said out loud.

"Turn here," Archer yelled out. "Her dot's at the end of this road."

"Wade, listen to me," Vince said sternly. "You are not going in half-cocked."

I started to growl and interrupt him, but he held up his hand.

"No, dude," he continued. "We have no idea what we're walking into. If he has a gun on her, you storming in there could make it worse. We have to do this the smart way. We *all* do this the smart way. Archer, text Ruthie our current location and have her send the cops here."

"I don't want the cops involved, because I will kill him if I find him," I snarled.

"Wade, why do you think we waited this long to give them our location?" Archer asked, and I knew what he wasn't saying. He'd done it this way to give us time to take care of it ourselves, or at least a decent head start.

We pulled up the drive but stopped short so no one heard our vehicle. As we got out of the car quietly, we saw two cars—one that looked like Beth's blue Corolla and a black SUV with Tennessee tags. This was it.

"Beth's here," I told them. "That's her blue car."

"Okay, we don't know for sure, but it appears she's in collusion with him, so we need to be careful of both of them," Archer said, always being the voice of reason, which I desperately needed at this moment. "Here are some comms," he said, handing us earpieces. "Do you both have weapons?"

"Yes." I usually didn't carry it while working at the

pub, but since I was upstairs in the security office, I hadn't taken it off yet. Not that I needed one—the Rangers had trained me to be deadly enough with just my hands and body.

"Yeah, I do," Vince replied. "Her dot's definitely in that building."

"Let's go," I said as I opened the door to get out.

We closed the doors as quietly as we could, then started moving toward the house. Archer whispered in the comms he'd go around to the back of the house to check for alternate exits. Vince and I went up to the front. As we got to the front door, I heard a man yell in what sounded like agony. Vince signaled me that he had my cover and to try the front door. It opened freely, which was not a good sign. If the bastard wasn't worried about Ellie escaping out an unlocked door, then she must be restrained.

The first thing I saw was Beth. Her prone body was on the floor and there was a lot of blood under her. I signaled to Vince, and he covered me while I crouched down to check for a pulse. There wasn't one, which didn't surprise me, given the amount of blood and the gunshot wound to her head. I whispered quietly in my comms to alert Archer that Beth was DOA (dead on arrival). I started to stand back up, when I heard a scream and recognized that voice to be Ellie's. My entire body stilled, and I felt chills on every inch of my skin.

I started to move toward the sound, when I felt Vince grab my arm. He signaled for me to stay slow and quiet. I knew the only thing we had going for us right now was the element of surprise. We needed to maintain that since Beth was already dead and we didn't want to add Ellie to that list.

We quickly but quietly stalked down the hallway to the right where the noises were coming from.

The long hallway appeared to be lined with bedrooms and bathrooms. We came up to the last one on the left, and what I saw would haunt me for the rest of my life. A man's body on top of Ellie's, with his hand on her neck, suffocating her. I knew it wasn't the smartest move tactically, but I launched myself at him, ripped him off her, and threw him to the ground. I pinned him there and got several good, hard punches into his head before Vince grabbed my arm.

"I got him. Go check Ellie," he said sternly.

I released the dickhead and turned around for Ellie. I would never forget how she looked in that moment. Tears on her face, her neck covered in red finger marks, and her arms tied to the bed. She was gasping for air but looking right at me, and then her eyes closed.

"Ellie, wake up, sweetheart," I told her, putting my hand on her cheek and trying to get her to open her eyes again.

I vaguely noted Vince talking behind me but didn't register what he was saying or who he was even talking to.

Ellie wasn't responding to my pleading to open her

eyes, and I didn't want to shake her in order to wake her because I didn't know the extent of her injuries.

Just then, Archer appeared next. "An ambulance is on the way."

"She won't open her eyes. I can't get her to open them," I told him, frantically hoping he could help me.

"She might have passed out from shock," he said to me calmly, putting his hand on my shoulder. "If she's still breathing and has a pulse, she's okay. Let's cut those off her wrists."

He pulled out his pocketknife, and worked delicately to remove the ropes from her wrists. I quickly cataloged any other injuries she may have had and then picked her up and proceeded to carry her down the hallway so I could get her on the ambulance as soon as they arrived. I left Archer and Vince in the room to deal with that asshole. I didn't even care at this point if he lived or died. I would kill him myself right now, but Ellie was my priority, and she needed me. I carried her bridal-style out of the house just as an officer was getting out of his car.

I yelled, "She needs medical attention immediately!"

He pointed over his shoulder. "The EMTs are right behind me."

I looked up to see the ambulance pulling up to the house. "Two of my guys are in there with the suspect on the ground, and there's a body just inside the front door."

The EMTs got out of the ambulance, and they met me as I strode toward them.

I quickly explained her injuries, at least the ones I

knew about, as I moved to put her on the stretcher myself. "He was strangling her when we got here. There's a handprint on her face, so he must have slapped her, and she's got a big knot on the back of her head."

The first EMT tried to wave me away and tell me which hospital they were transporting her to, but I hopped into the back. I wasn't leaving her side for one minute. The man either understood or was too scared to argue with me in my current mood, so he climbed in, closed the doors, and we took off.

While the EMT assessed her, I pulled out my phone to text Archer and Vince, letting them know I was going to the hospital with her.

The ride took less than ten minutes, but it felt like one of the longest rides of my life. I took her hand in mine, gently rubbing the marks on her wrist where that bastard had tied her up.

I felt her hand move under mine and looked up to find her eyes on me—filled with tears. She wasn't sobbing, but she was clearly experiencing an emotional dump now that her adrenaline rush had worn off.

"Hey, baby," I tried to say calmly, trying to remove all murderous thoughts about her ex so I didn't scare her.

"It's really you," she rasped and then coughed a little.

"Try not to talk too much until we can check out your throat," the EMT said. "We want to make sure your larynx, trachea, and vocal cords weren't damaged."

She nodded back and then moved her eyes to me and gave me a small smile.

"You're safe now," I told her, and I moved my hand from her wrist to her hand and squeezed it gently.

My words registered to her, and then it appeared she began to think back to what had happened before I got there, and the fear returned to her eyes.

"Randall," she whispered.

"Ma'am, please try not to talk until we get there," the EMT reminded her politely.

"Don't worry about Randall, baby. He's not going to be a problem anymore," I told her, putting my free hand on her cheek. "You're safe now. We just need to get you checked out at the hospital."

She nodded and continued to stare into my eyes until the heaviness took over and she fell asleep. The EMT assured me it was fine to let her sleep, as her vitals were improving.

I had to believe him because I couldn't lose her now.

24

JACK

Not that I expected a welcome party at the airport, but I did assume someone would have been there to pick me up. After countless phone calls and texts to Vince, Wade, Ellie, and Archer all went unanswered, I finally decided to take a cab back to my apartment.

I continued to try to reach out to everyone for the hour drive home, but no one responded.

When we pulled up to the front of my building, the first thing I noticed was several police vehicles with lights on. As I walked to the main door to the building, I saw the officers in the front lobby of Ranger Shield Security.

This couldn't be good. I wondered if this was why no one answered my calls. My original plan was to head straight to my apartment, but now I found myself entering the reception area.

I walked in to find a young woman with silver-blonde hair directing the cops, her voice sharp with urgency. A tall man stood at her back, his posture tense, as if ready to intervene if needed.

She was stunning. Her hair bounced as she turned back and forth, issuing instructions to the officers in the room. There was fire in her eyes—not arrogance, but determination. I suspected she was Ruthie, our reception-ist, though having never met her, I couldn't be sure.

Not seeing anyone else I recognized, I decided to speak up, introduce myself, and find out what was going on.

"Excuse me," I said, but her voice carried over mine, unwavering.

The man at her back was the only one to take notice of me, though he remained silent. I tried again, louder this time.

"Excuse me—can someone tell me what's going on?"

This time, she turned, her gaze sharp and slightly annoyed as it landed on me. "Listen here shitwhistle, I don't know who you are, but you can't be here right now."

I felt my eyes widen in shock as well as my lips twitch as I thought about what she called me. This woman was a firecracker.

"Ruthie, I think this guy…" the taller man beside her started, confirming my suspicion about her identity.

"This guy can wait, Diego," she said firmly, cutting him off.

Ah, so this must be Diego, the new hire the guys had mentioned. I assumed he may know who I was so I nodded to him. He tried to interrupt, but before he could speak again, she continued.

"Every minute we waste answering his questions," she said, pointing at me, "is a minute that could be used to help the cops find Ellie."

Wait. Did she just say my sister's name? I decided I'd had enough letting the little firecracker take over the conversation.

"Ellie Hutchinson?" I asked. "What happened to Ellie?" my voice got louder, and I moved back closer to the cops.

"Sir, if you," one of the cops tried to interrupt me but I wasn't having it.

"That's my sister. I'm Jack Hutchinson, her brother. What happened, officer?" I demanded.

The room went silent as everyone stared at me.

"I'm Diego Martin, new hire," he reached out to shake my hand.

"Heard about you, nice to meet you. Can you tell me what's going on?" I shook his hand and asked him.

Diego, along with two of the officers filled me in on what little they knew about my sister being kidnapped. They mentioned Ruthie had given Ellie a tracker, which they were using to find her.

Throughout the conversation, Ruthie had been silent —a stark contrast to her previous firecracker attitude.

"They found her," one of the cops announced from the corner of the room while on his phone.

At the same time, my phone buzzed in my pocket. I pulled it out to see Vince's name on the screen.

"I'm at the office and have been briefed on Ellie being kidnapped," I announced. "Sitrep?"

"We found her. She's alive and on her way to the hospital with Wade. Relay to Diego and Ruthie. One of them can drive you. I'll meet you there."

He hung up and I noticed he said she was alive but didn't give any details as to how badly she was injured. I didn't waste time. I relayed what I heard from Vince to the room.

"I'm coming with you," Ruthie decreed.

"I'll stay here and handle whatever the cops need," Diego added.

"That's fine, but I don't have my car keys on me." I assumed they were still in my apartment somewhere, but I hadn't even been up there yet.

"I'll drive, let's go," Ruthie replied.

Not that I didn't appreciate the offer, but she was clearly emotional and likely not in the best state to drive. Diego must have sensed that too.

"That's Dane and Axel walking in behind you," Diego told me. "They're our brand-new hires. Dane can drive you, and Axel can stay here to assist with the cops."

"Fine, let's go," Ruthie agreed, before quickly walking toward the door.

I slid into the passenger seat as Ruthie hopped in behind Dane. I could hear her sniffles few times before she broke her silence.

"I'm sorry," she said quietly.

"Ruthie, this isn't your fault, get that shit out of your mind," Dane responded.

"I didn't mean it that way," she said.

I turned my head to look at her and she was staring right at me.

"I was a total bitch to you. I'm sorry," her voice hitched. "It's just that your sister is the only friend I've made since moving here and I was really stressed out. When you barged in, I just assumed you were some rando looking for a job or something."

"I get it," I told her. "I would have done the same thing for my friends too. I'm happy Ellie has you. Especially since it sounds like the necklace charm was your doing. I should be thanking you."

She nodded but didn't say anything else. The rest of the ride was quiet as we made our way to the hospital.

My priorities when we got there would be to know that my sister would be okay, and to find out if her ex was dead. Because if he wasn't, he would be soon.

25

WADE

It took only minutes to get to the hospital, but it felt so much longer. When we arrived, I tried to follow the EMT's back with the stretcher but was told I needed to go to a waiting room while they checked her over. The only reason I didn't throw a huge fit was because the EMT assured me she would be fine as we exited the vehicle.

A nurse walked me over to a small waiting room and asked me some basic questions about Ellie then told me to wait there for information from the doctor.

"Can I just wait in the room she'll go in after she is done being examined?" I asked, knowing it was a long shot. "I'm her fiancé," I threw in at the end for good measure, knowing family got more privileges than just friends.

"We don't know what room she'll go in yet, but I promise to come give you any information I can when I know," she said kindly and smiled at me. Then, she turned and walked out of the small waiting room as I reached for my phone.

I needed to check in with Archer and Vince, and I might as well do it while I waited.

"Hey man, where are you?" Vince asked with not much of a greeting.

"I'm at the hospital, sitting in the waiting room while they check her over," I told him.

"I know that, but where exactly?" he pressed. "I'm here too with one of the officers. They need to get your statement."

I told him my waiting room location and then hung up, knowing they would be here momentarily. I didn't want to do this, but I'd rather get this over with now so that when they called me back to go see Ellie, I wasn't tied up in the middle of it.

Vince walked in moments later with an older-looking cop.

"Sir, my name is Officer Teller. Do you mind if we go in that more private room over there?" the officer asked me and pointed to the other side of the waiting room, where there was what appeared to be a smaller room with a table and four chairs.

"I'd prefer we stay here in case the doctor comes out, if you don't mind," I explained to him.

"Go, dude. If the doctor comes out, I'll come get you, I'll stay put right here," Vince said, trying to assure me.

I nodded and followed the officer into the small room. I answered all his questions about how we came upon the scene and what happened after. Twenty minutes later, I walked out to find not only Vince, but also Ruthie, Dane, and Jack.

Shit. I had totally forgotten Jack was arriving tonight. Talk about terrible timing. But my first words were to Vince, not Jack.

"Anything?" I asked him.

"Not a word," he said.

I sighed and ran my hand over my face, part relieved I didn't miss anything, but also frustrated that they hadn't been out to tell us what was going on. I turned to see Jack stroll up to me.

"Shit circumstances, but glad to see you, man, and really glad you were there to help tonight," Jack said as he walked over to me, and grabbed my hand, and pulled me in for our usual half shake, half hug.

"Where's my girl?" I heard yelled from across the room, and I looked up to see Tammy prowling in like she was on a mission and would kill anyone who got in her way.

She was closely followed by Chuck, who looked calm as a cucumber, but I knew that was only on the surface. His tightened fists and hard eyes told another story. Tammy came straight to me.

"How is she? Where's Beth? Did you kill that asshole ex of hers? What room is she in? I want to go see her," she asked in rapid fire, but before I could even attempt to answer any of them, a doctor came into the room.

"Elliana Hutchinson?" the doctor said to the room.

Almost every one of us in the room spoke up to let the doctor know we were all here for her. The doctor gave a small smile and looked at all of us.

"She has multiple contusions on her neck, face, and wrists," the doctor explained. "There's swelling around her neck, and while her voice is raspy, there appears to be no permanent damage to her vocal cords. She also suffered a mild concussion from the blow to the head. She's awake now, but we can only let one person back at a time. We'll start with her fiancé." He looked at me, and I assumed the nurse must have passed along my fiancé comment to him. "Then the rest of you can come back one at a time only, please."

"*Her what?*" Jack almost yelled as I got up and went to follow the doctor. "Wait. I'm her brother I'd like to see her," he told the doctor and started to walk to the door.

"She's asked for her fiancé first, so let's start with him, and then you can go back," the doctor explained calmly.

She asked for her fiancé? I knew I'd used that term in hopes it would get me extra access to her, but why had she used it?

I could feel Jack glaring at me behind my back. I needed to talk to him about Ellie, but I wanted to talk to her first. The need to see her myself and know that she was okay was a higher priority than talking to Jack at the moment.

The doctor and I cleared the door as I heard Jack ask Vince what the hell was going on. I felt a little bad for Vince because I was sure he wasn't thrilled at having to be the one to tell Jack I'd been seeing his sister and no one had told him.

"Her bruises are starting to set in," the doctor explained to me as we walked down the hallway. "And the marks are going to be more pronounced than when you brought her in, so just be prepared. The cops would like to speak with her, but I'll hold them off for a little bit so you can visit with her privately." He pointed to the room on the right, and I thanked him before opening the door and going inside.

I walked in quietly and noticed her eyes were closed. I took the moment to just look her over as I walked a little closer to her bed. Despite all the marks on her body and bruises starting to appear, she was still the most beautiful thing I'd ever seen. But God, seeing her broken like this tore me up. Guilt, sadness, and anger battled inside me, along with so much more. I closed my eyes and took a few deep breaths to calm myself.

"I hear my *fiancé* Wade came in with me," she said softly and a bit raspy as I opened my eyes to see her looking at me. "You wouldn't happen to know anything about that would you, *fiancé*?" The grin on her face grew.

"I'll admit, it may have started as a white lie to give me access to you that I otherwise wouldn't have had, but mark my words, babe, one day you *will* wear my ring and that fiancé comment will no longer be anything but the truth."

She gasped, and I saw tears start filling up in her eyes. I decided to go for it and tell her everything so she knew I was serious. Because when her brother walked in, I wanted us all to be on the same page.

"You own me, Ellie—lock, stock, and barrel," I told her. "You're the best thing that's ever happened to me, and I can't lose you. Even with all the battles I fought overseas, I have never felt fear penetrate so deep inside me like it did when I walked into that room and saw that fucker on top of you, choking you."

I took a few breaths, trying to calm myself down because the last thing I needed was to scare her with my anger.

"Come here," she said, reaching out.

I walked toward her and took her hand in mine, leaning down to cup her cheek with my other hand.

"I love you, Wade Watson," she told me softly with a smile gleaming on her face.

Damn. Those words. In that moment, I vowed to myself to do whatever it took to never see this brave and beautiful woman in this state again. I would show her how much she meant to me every day for the rest of my life.

"I love you too, baby," I told her and then leaned forward to kiss her. I wanted to kiss her hard, but I knew I had to be gentle because of her injuries.

"The hell are you doing to my sister?" Jack growled behind me, but before I could fully turn around, another voice spoke up.

"Move it, young man. I need to see my girl, and your

big head is blocking me," Tammy all but hollered at Jack, using her arms to shove her way around him.

Tammy gasped loudly when she saw Ellie and then her face turned red.

"Tell me one of y'all killed him," she snarled.

"I'm okay, Tammy," Ellie told her with a small smile on her face.

"You will be, girl. You will be," Tammy said, shaking her head.

26

ELLIE

I looked up and realized it wasn't just Tammy and Jack in the room with Wade and me, but others I've come to know the past few months were also here. Chuck and Vince were behind my brother, along with one of the new guys who were just hired at the security firm, though I couldn't place his name. Then I heard a sniffle, and I saw Ruthie standing next to Jack as she looked at me.

"Hey Ruthie, I'm gonna be okay, I promise," I said, hoping it would ease her concerns.

"Damn right she will be," Tammy interrupted. "Especially after I get my hands on that bitch Beth and wring her neck."

A deep cough, meant to get attention, came in from behind the group. I looked up and saw Archer with a man next to him I didn't recognize.

"Elliana, my name is Detective Cooper," the man said,

and only then did I notice the badge on his belt. "I'd like to ask you some questions if you're feeling up to it."

Wade leaned down and spoke to me softly, taking my hand. "You don't have to do this right now if you're not up to it."

"It's okay. I'd rather get it over with so I don't have to think about it again." I squeezed his hand to reassure him.

"Please call me Ellie," I said to the detective and told him to ask what he needed to.

He told me to start from the beginning right before I was grabbed.

I explained about Beth telling me that Wade needed me, and we'd gone outside. As Beth and I had walked out the door, something hit my head, and the next thing I remembered, I was waking up in the house with my hands tied to the headboard.

I continued, and there were several gasps from the women and several growls from the men when I gave specific details, but the part that seemed to bother all of them the most was anything to do with Beth. Everyone was upset to find out she'd been helping Randall the whole time.

"Beth said you two had a connection," I said, looking at Wade.

"That's a crock of..." Wade interrupted, shaking his head. "We never went out, and I never gave her any indication I was interested."

"I know," I said, squeezing his hand to try to calm him

down. "She said you two were getting close and were going to be lovers if I hadn't stepped in. She said when she saw us getting close, she had to get rid of me."

I explained how all the things that had been done to my car—the radio, the moved seats and mirrors, and the air freshener were all done by Beth. She would take my car keys out of my purse while I was at work, go change something in my car, and come back before her break was over.

Even after I told them that Randall had shot her, the only response was from Chuck, who muttered, "Good riddance bitch." I got to the part about Randall's other confession and started to cry. I looked at my brother and could barely even mutter the words.

"He killed Gran," I told him. I turned to the sergeant and told him the details, trying not to cry through it, even though it broke my heart to know that she died because of me. Had I not dated Randall, she never would have died when she did.

"I'll kill that motherfucker," Jack groaned, not loudly, but loud enough that the sergeant looked over at him.

"That won't be necessary," Archer said from the back of the room.

"Did you arrest him?" I asked the sergeant, needing to know if I would have to testify.

"He didn't make it, Miss Hutchinson," Detective Cooper said.

I was sure the confused look on my face was obvious. I

felt Wade's hand squeeze mine, and I looked up at him. His face held no emotion and was entirely unreadable. I looked back at the sergeant.

"What do you mean?" I asked.

"The injuries he sustained from Mr. Watson and Mr. Fletcher as they were restraining him from attacking you were too much, and he was pronounced dead by the EMTs on the way to the hospital," Detective Cooper said.

This was news to me. I remembered Randall on top of me choking me, and then he was gone. Then I saw Wade's face, but everything after that was a bit fuzzy.

"Are you arresting Wade and Vince?" I asked the sergeant, panic starting to build in me at the thought of them being taken away.

"Not at this time, no," he said. "While perhaps a bit aggressive, it appears he fought back, so the injuries he sustained from Watson and Fletcher are from self-defense and protecting you."

I sighed as relief washed through me. Then it hit me how tired I was. I didn't realize I had closed my eyes until I heard Wade's voice.

"Enough questions for now. She needs to rest," he said.

"It's okay, I think I have everything I need," Detective Cooper said. "If you think of anything else, please give me a call." He handed me his card and then walked out of the room.

I tried hard to keep my eyes open, but then Wade

leaned down, brushed a kiss on my forehead, and whispered, "Sleep, baby. I'll be here when you wake up."

I gave up resisting and closed my eyes, letting sleep pull me under.

When I woke later, the only people still in my room were Wade, Vince, Ruthie, and Jack.

"How did you find me?" I asked Wade and Vince. "Did you follow Beth? I was worried you wouldn't be able to find me because I hadn't taken my phone, but you found me."

Neither of them said a word for a moment, and just as Wade started to open his mouth, Ruthie interrupted.

"It was actually me. I'm sorry, Ellie. I just wanted to do my part to keep you safe."

The confusion on my face must have been easy to read, because she exhaled and took a step forward.

"The boxing glove charm I gave you," she explained nervously. "It has a tracker on it. Mine does too. Archer gave it to me when we moved here, just in case something happened. When I heard about your ex, I told him I wanted to get you one too, so we did."

She sighed then stepped closer to me. "I'm sorry I didn't tell you. I couldn't think of the right way to say it, and then I let it go for so long that I was worried you would be upset I didn't tell you, so I just kept it to myself."

I nodded, understanding what she was saying and so

thankful that she had the foresight to do that. I then looked at Wade assuming he would say something, but Ruthie spoke again.

"Don't blame Wade. He didn't know," she said, jumping to his defense. "Only Archer and I knew. And Archer thought I'd told you, and he figured if you wanted Wade to know, that you would tell him. He didn't know I hadn't told you. I'm so sorry."

She tilted her head down almost in defeat, and I felt bad that she felt so guilty over something that ultimately saved my life.

"Ruthie, I'm not mad," I emphasized. "Just before the guys arrived, Randall was choking me and likely would have killed me. If you hadn't given me that, the guys may not have made it in time. I'm not even a little mad. I'm thrilled you gave me that charm. Thank you for saving my life."

She burst into tears, and my brother suddenly grabbed her by the shoulder and pulled her into him, whispering something in her ear as he rubbed his hand up and down her back.

Before I could ask anything else, a nurse I hadn't seen before walked in. The look on her face showed she was clearly surprised to see so many people in the room, and she wasn't having it.

"Okay, then, all of you. If you aren't family, out of the room, now," she demanded and clapped her hands twice to get them going.

Vince gave me a quick nod and then left, but Wade,

Jack, and also Ruthie, who was currently attached to my brother's side, stayed put.

"Who are all of you?" the nurse asked, clearly making a stand about the family only rule.

"I'm her fiancé," Wade answered, and my mouth turned into a small smile at his little white lie.

The nurse turned to my brother and Ruthie and lifted her eyebrow, clearly wanting to know who they were.

"I'm her brother, and this is *my fiancé*," Jack said with a little snark emphasizing on the last two words, making it clear to us that if Wade could lie about a fiancé, so could he.

"Okay, then, you three. Over there on the side while I check her, and then you can have your time with her," the nurse said, pointing to the other side of the room, and then she came to me to check all my vitals. "How are you feeling, dear?" Her voice had instantly softened from the snippy one she'd given everyone else in the room.

"A little sleepy but good," I told her.

"Pain management okay?" she asked, and I nodded in return.

She wrote a few things down on her chart and then told my family they had thirty minutes and then I needed to rest. I smiled because she reminded me a little of Tammy.

Wanting to lighten the mood a little between the two broody men standing in my room, I turned to my brother to tease him a little.

"Not sure you can give Wade any crap for getting a

fiancé since you have one too apparently," I said with a smirk.

"Yeah, well, if this loser is allowed to use that fake excuse to see you, then so can I in order for Ruthie to stay," he explained while glaring at Wade.

"It won't be a fake excuse for long," Wade said to my brother, then walked up to my bed and grabbed my hand in his squeezing gently.

The mood in the room electrified, and I saw the change on my brother's face before he spoke.

"Care to explain?" he asked with purpose to Wade and began to untangle himself from Ruthie, but she latched onto his arm to try to hold him in place.

"Your sister and I have been seeing each other," Wade said, eyes straight on Jack's. "I was going to tell you when you got back, but it got serious before I even realized." He looked down at me. "I love her." He smiled at me then looked back to Jack. "I get this might be a shock, and I'm sorry I didn't tell you sooner, but hopefully you can understand we were a little busy with the other priority of keeping her safe."

"I was going to tell you when you got back too. Everything," I told my brother. "Not just about Wade, but everything with Randall too. I just didn't want to worry you and add to your stress while you were on your final mission. I'm sorry, big brother."

The tension in Jack's face that had been aimed at Wade now softened as he looked to me.

"You happy?" Jack asked me softly.

"I am now," I said, and I realized I genuinely meant it. I looked up at Wade and smiled at him, and he winked back.

"You hurt her, and I'll kill you. Don't care if you're my friend or not," Jack said to Wade with a stoic look on his face.

"I'll hand you the gun myself," Wade responded back.

I decided to change the topic to get some answers.

"I'm sorry this is our reunion, but I'm happy to see you," I told Jack. "Did the guys call you and tell you to come here?"

"I realized something was wrong when no one was answering their phones to come pick me up from the airport," he started to say. "I got an cab to bring me to my apartment, and when I got there, there were multiple squad cars. I walked into the Ranger Shield Security front office and saw Ruthie here explaining to the cops about the security cameras in our building. Once I introduced myself to the cops, everyone got me up to speed. Then Vince called me back a few minutes later and let me know they'd found you and more of the details."

"I'm so sorry," I said to Jack, feeling terrible that this was what he came home to.

"Don't apologize," he said. "I'm happy you're safe, that asshole is dead, and I'm happy you moved down here. That's all that matters for now."

He was right. That was all that mattered. I was so happy he was home safe from his latest mission—even happier it was his last. Happy to be making new friends, starting school soon, and happy to have Wade in my life.

Wade squeezed my hand and leaned down to kiss my head, and I felt so completely content for the first time in a long time.

Here's to a new beginning, I thought, looking over at the people who meant so much to me.

I was walking into the entrance to Ranger Shield when I saw my sister coming out of the elevator and heading in the direction of the front office—the same place I was going. She was dressed for her shift at the pub in her T-shirt and jeans. This was her first shift back since getting out of the hospital.

"Hey sis. You feeling okay?" I asked because I wasn't sure she should be going back to work so soon.

"Yes, Dad," she said, rolling her eyes at me. "I'm good, and I'm ready to go back to work. Plus, Wade is working with me tonight, which means I won't have any heavy lifting to do."

That only eased my concern a little bit, but before I could argue with her more about it, she walked into the front office and headed to Ruthie's desk.

Ruthie and Wade were standing over her desk going over some papers when we walked in. Ruthie was a mystery to me. I had met her when I arrived to chaos after Ellie was taken. She was gorgeous but guarded. I'd tried to get to know her better since I came home, but she was always professional and never deviated into anything remotely resembling interest.

Plus, I got the impression she and Archer either were together now or had been in the past, so I didn't want to get into that, until I had more information. If I was wrong, however, and neither of those were true, then I would definitely try to find a way to break through her guarded exterior.

Ruthie intrigued me more than anyone I'd ever met, and I wasn't about to let assumptions stand in the way of discovering who she really was. I'd bide my time, be patient, and look for the right moment to insert myself into her life.

"Hi, Ruthie," Ellie said, waving at her, but she walked over to Wade.

He pulled her into his arms and kissed her deeply.

I heard a growling noise and quickly realized it had come from me. Ruthie chuckled and it lit up her face, even though she was trying to hide the fact that she'd laughed.

Ellie said goodbye and headed off to the restaurant for her shift.

"See you in a few, baby," Wade yelled to her as she left.

I turned my head back to him and gave him my best deadly glare.

"You gonna keep my sister living in sin in your apartment, or are you gonna make an honest woman out of her anytime soon?" I grilled Wade.

"I've already got the ring. Just waiting for the right moment to ask," Wade responded quickly and with a grin on his face.

I was surprised by that statement, but deep down a part of me was happy he wasn't just using her to make another notch in his bedpost.

"She doesn't have a dad anymore, but she has you," Wade said, his face more serious now.

I knew what he was going to ask. For permission to marry my sister. Wade was a good man. He was a great sergeant to me while overseas, an even better friend, and I knew he would be good for my sister. But I still wanted to make him squirm a little.

"Yeah, and I'm all she needs," I told him, trying to keep a straight face.

His face twitched ever so slightly. I imagined most people would have missed it, but you learned to watch your brothers' faces because sometimes you couldn't speak on a mission, so you relied on hand signals and facial expressions to communicate. Just as quickly as that twitch was there, it was gone, though, and determination took over.

"Not anymore," he told me. "I'm here for the long haul, and I'd like your permission to marry her. Not because I need it, but because it will make her happy."

The look on his face said he was asking, but he was going to marry her anyway, regardless of what I said.

"I don't care that we're brothers," I said to Wade with such intensity, it made him squirm a bit. "You hurt her, I will kill you and bury the body where no one will find it, and we both know I'm capable of that."

"Don't be a dick," a little voice popped up.

I realized it was Ruthie, and she was staring right at me. Then she walked over to Wade, standing in front of him as though she was protecting him. All five foot nothing of her. I glanced up at Wade, who was grinning, likely thinking the same thing I was. It was funny that she thought he needed her protection. Even funnier that the protector would be her. This woman was something else.

"Alright, just so you don't break a nail attempting to save Wade from me, I'll give," I told Ruthie, grinning at her before turning to Wade. "You have my permission. Guess we'll actually get to be real brothers then."

I extended my hand to him. He grinned at me, grabbed my hand, and then pulled me in for a shoulder grasp.

"Here's to a new beginning," Wade said, and I internally smiled, happy that my sister finally had that.

EPILOGUE
ELLIE

There were moments in life that you didn't want to end. You wanted to savor every detail, capturing them in your memory so that you could look back on them later and smile. This was one of those moments.

Wade, my now-husband, was sitting in our rocking chair with our eight-month-old baby girl Maya. Much to my mother-in-law's anguish, we had not continued the trend of names that started with W, though once she'd laid eyes on Maya, she'd said it didn't matter and instead lavished her with copious amounts of Grandma snuggles.

Wade sat there, whispering to Maya as he tried to lull her to sleep. She, however, continued blabbering away to him, as if they were having the most intense conversation. He hummed in response, nodding seriously, as if she were telling him the secrets of the universe. I still couldn't believe I got to call this man my husband.

As soon as I left the hospital after I was attacked, I

moved in with Wade permanently. He hadn't given me much of a choice. He insisted that my only priority should be recovering fully—not worrying about finding another place yet.

A few months later, we were getting ready to go have another Sunday meal with his family, when he walked into the bedroom doorway, leaning into the frame, and stared at me while I put the last touches of my makeup on.

"You going to stare at me the whole time I get ready?" I asked him while I put mascara on.

"I love looking at you," he said with a lustful grin on his face.

"I know that look. Don't you dare come in here and mess up my hair and makeup," I warned, knowing if I let him, he would throw me on the bed and have his way with me, all while messing up my hair and makeup.

"It would be worth it." His grin turned into a lascivious smile. *"But I'm actually staring because you're missing something."*

I turned to look at myself in the mirror, scanning myself top to bottom, and tried to see what I was missing. Not seeing anything, I turned back to him, only to see him drop to one knee with a small box in his hands.

"You are the best thing that has ever happened to me," Wade said as I felt my eyes get wet and blurry. *"I know I don't deserve you and I am definitely marrying up, but I promise you I will show you every single day for the rest of our lives how much I love you. Ellie, will you marry me?"*

The ring was absolutely beautiful. I nodded, too choked up at first to speak, and then said yes, though I wasn't sure he understood what I was saying through all my happy tears.

He picked me up and carried me to the bed, and I ended up having to do my hair and makeup all over again.

He told me he proposed at that moment so the females in his family wouldn't gang up on him during the meal, nagging him about when he was going to propose and why it was taking him so long. Apparently this had been happening the last few meals when I was in another room.

His plan backfired, though, because while the women were all very excited and ready to talk wedding plans, his mom and grandma jumped right into nagging him about another topic—grandbabies and great-grandbabies.

They didn't have to wait too long for that either, though. Just six months later, on our wedding night, after all the festivities were over—we'd had the ceremony in his parents' backyard garden and the reception at the pub, which we'd closed off for the night for friends and family only—he made love to me for the first time as husband and wife. He was lying there on his back, fully satisfied in the bed, when I climbed back in next to him. I had a picture in my hands behind my back—the ultrasound picture I had gotten the day before.

"I have a present for you," I said softly.

"Mmm...I liked the present you just gave me....wife," he replied, grinning lasciviously at me.

I laughed softly and slowly handed him the picture. At first, he looked at it like he was unsure of what he was looking at. Then his eyes moved to me, then back to the picture, then back to me.

"Jesus, Ellie. You are the best thing that has ever happened to me," he said softly and reverently before kissing me hard. "There was a time when I had made peace with the fact that I would likely never be in a relationship again and never get the chance to have a family. Now, you've given me both."

He put the picture on the nightstand and turned to cup my face in his hands. "God, Ellie, I love you so much."

Now, months later, I looked at him in the rocker, our baby girl nestled in his arms, and wished I could freeze this moment forever. It was a picture of pure contentment, one I never wanted to end.

After a few more moments, Wade gently stood from the chair and placed Maya back in her crib. He lingered for a second, adjusting her tiny blanket, and my heart squeezed.

Then, turning to me, he reached for my hands. "Come with me, my beautiful wife," he murmured, his voice low and warm as he pulled me toward the door.

I let him lead me out of Maya's room. "Where are you taking me, handsome husband?" I whispered back.

"To our room, so I can put another baby inside you," he said, a playful smirk curling at the corners of his mouth before he leaned down to kiss me.

That kiss turned into something deeper. And sure

enough, just shy of ten months later, our son Rowan was born.

That day in Tennessee that changed my life forever felt like a lifetime ago. While the memory of what I went through is difficult, it led me to my wonderful husband and our two beautiful children. My life was now better than I had ever imagined, and I thanked my lucky stars every day for the blessings I have.

Thank you for reading *Betrayal And New Beginnings*.
I hope you enjoyed it.

The Ranger Shield Security Series continues with the story of Vince & Catalina in *Instinct & New Identity*.

BUY INSTINCT & NEW IDENTITY NOW
at www.AllisonBettes.com

To find out when new books release
SIGN UP FOR MY NEWSLETTER today at
www.AllisonBettes.com.

Keep reading for a sneak peek of *Instinct & New Identity*...

INSTINCT & NEW IDENTITY

SNEAK PEEK AT THE NEXT RANGER SHIELD
SECURITY NOVEL

The Ranger Shield Security Series continues with the story of Vince & Catalina in *Instinct & New Identity*.

Catalina "Cat" Rivera's life is upended after a gas station robbery claims her parents' lives and forces her and her younger sister into Witness Protection. Seven years later, the quiet life Cat has worked hard to build is shattered when Vince Fletcher, her former military pen pal, tracks her down. Once bound by letters exchanged during Vince's deployment, their connection reignites. But Vince's arrival stirs up more than memories—it threatens to unravel the safety net Cat has carefully constructed. While Vince offers protection and an opportunity for a fresh start with his Georgia-based security firm, Cat must confront her lingering fear, unresolved grief, and burgeoning feelings for the man who never forgot her. As past and present collide, Cat and Vince navigate old dangers and new emotions. Together, they face not only the potential exposure of Cat's hidden identity but also a new threat from a target neither of them ever considered. While navigating a world where trust is a perilous choice, Cat must decide whether Vince can have a place in her life as she faces the looming threats to herself and her sister.

Turn the page to read a sneak preview.

Dear soldier,

First, thank you for your service. I'm writing to you as part of our school project to write to a soldier and admittedly I don't know what to say. We aren't allowed to tell you our name or anything identifiable about ourselves, so that kind of restricts what I usually write about. So I apologize in advance if you find this boring, but hopefully not :)

I'm 17 years old (about to turn 18), female, and a senior in high school in Florida. I have a younger sister who is 13 and a total pain in my butt. My favorite classes are art and technology. I'm hoping to go to college next year for coding or computer science (nerd alert).

Without writing your name or "anything identifiable" tell me about yourself. Do you have any siblings? What do you like to do? Any hobbies?

In an effort to make this not completely boring here's a joke (that hopefully isn't too cheesy).

Why did the soldier bring a pen into battle?

(because he wanted to draw his weapon – ha!)

Hope you have a great day!

—C

Hey C,

Thanks for writing. We get a lot of letters, and trust me, yours is not boring compared to most of the others. It must have been that cheesy dad-joke you added at the end ;)

I'm 20 years old, male, and from Georgia. I also have a younger sister who is a pain in my butt, though I would have chosen a different word to use for her. She's also a senior in high school, though she has no idea what she wants to go to school for.

When I'm not stuck in a giant sand box, I like to play video games, hang out with my friends, and watch sports. I like all sports, but football and soccer are my favorite to watch on tv. I enjoy crossword puzzles and word searches, and I also like to read suspense novels and biographies.

What about you? What do you do for fun?

I'm not an artist, so I won't attempt to draw a cute animal like you did, but here's my attempt at a cheesy joke.

What is a soldier's favorite holiday?

(Tanks-giving)

—V

Hi V,

Okay your joke was definitely cheesier than mine, but I still laughed. Did you say my cat was "cute"? I drew you a very tough and intimidating cat! In fact, that cat is so tough it will protect you while you are overseas protecting people like me :)

I'm assuming from your sand box comment that you aren't in the Navy. Are you allowed to tell me what branch of the military you are in?

That's cool your sister is the same age as me! Most of my friends don't know what they want to do after they graduate either, so she isn't alone.

What do I do for fun? I love music. I listen to a variety: pop, country, Latin, hip-hop, rock, etc. Though my favorite is Taylor Swift. Yes, I am a huge Swiftie. I've never seen her in concert, but hopefully on her next tour I can go see her somewhere. Do you like music?

Why does the Army soldier always carry a pencil?

(Because they're really good at drawing blanks –hehe)

—C

C,

First of all, I'm not sure we can be writing friends anymore. A Swiftie? Really? My sister is also a Swiftie and I'm sorry but one of you is more than enough for me. I'm more of a classic rock and alternative rock music fan, though I can also tolerate some country music depending on the artist. Though saying that, and I'll deny it if you ever tell my sister, but at this very moment I wouldn't even complain if I heard Taylor Swift playing in the background instead of constant gunfire.

Second, I'm not sure I would have used those words to describe your cat drawing, but I'll take your word for it :)

Third, terrible joke. I can't give too many details, but I can tell you that I am part of the Army. My dad and grandfather were Army too. This means no more of those terrible jokes unless they are at the expense of the other branches...like the one I put below.

What do you call a Marine with half a brain?

(Gifted—ha!)

—V

V,

I don't even know you that well, but it bothers me a lot that you can hear that much gunfire constantly (even if you are admitting you secretly love Taylor Swift music). I don't even know what a real gunshot sounds like, other than what it sounds like in the movies. I'm here if you want to talk about it. Not sure how I could help, but I'm here if you need to vent. Just know that people like me appreciate what you are doing over there, and my evil, scary cat drawing will help protect you.

We can also talk about other things. How about the other guys in your Army group? Are they nice? Did you know any of them before hand?

Why did the Navy's ship blush?

(Because it saw the ocean's bottom—hehe)

—C

C,

Ah so we've switched to dirty jokes now? I definitely have a few of those up my sleeve :)

I'm glad you've never heard gunshots in real life. I hope it stays that way. It's not always gunfire over here. Honestly, it's mostly hurry up and wait. I spend most of my time sitting very still waiting for something that may or may not happen. It's very boring. But I would prefer the boring if it means all my crew stays safe.

Speaking of which, it's called a squadron—the group of guys I'm with here, and they are great. Sometimes we are with other squadrons if we team up for a mission, but most times it is just us. My sergeant is awesome. Some of them are dicks, but I really ended up with a great one.

You mentioned in your first letter that you were turning 18 soon, did you have your birthday yet? I just had mine a few months ago. The guys made me a sand cupcake. Don't worry, I didn't eat it. My mom sent me some socks, which is oddly an amazing gift over here because it may be hot during the day, but it can get super cold at night.

What's a soldier's favorite type of exercise?

(Booty camp)

-V

V,

I hope you like the gift I sent in your care package this week. It's not much, but you said socks are great, so consider it a belated birthday gift from me!

Yes, I'm 18 now! Just last month. I don't really feel any different, but I guess that's because I'm still living at home and in school. Maybe it will feel differently when I'm off to college.

I'm glad the guys you are with are great, and even happier you have a great sergeant! Can you tell me more about the guys (without giving too much away)?

Speaking of which, this writing program ends once I graduate, but I would really like to keep writing to you. I know sharing addresses for writing isn't really allowed, but what about email? Would you be open to that? No pressure if you don't. I just really enjoy our letters and feel a strange connection to you, and I'd like to keep in touch.

What form is required for all soldiers?

(A uni-form)

-C

C,

Ok, this is officially the worst gift ever. Taylor Swift socks?! Really?! Just so you know the guys in my squad gave me so much crap for these and will likely never let me live this down. Thanks a lot (huge eyeroll).

I'm only wearing them because they are thick and warm and the pair my mom sent me have a hole. Otherwise, these would be in the trash. After I burned them.

The only reason why I'm still even writing to you after

that horrible gift is because you also sent a crossword puzzle book. I've never done a murder mystery crossword before. This is actually a badass gift. You are forgiven for the awful socks. Barely.

Congratulations on almost graduating! I would definitely like to keep writing to you. Despite the bad jokes, and awful socks, your letters are a bright spot for me. Maybe it's because of the anonymity, but I feel like I can tell you anything. My email is below. Though fair warning, this may cause us to cross a line since you are now going to know part of my name.

What rank are all cats in the military?

(Corpurrrral)

V

VEFletcher123@gmail.com

Want more?

BUY INSTINCT & NEW IDENTITY NOW

at www.AllisonBettes.com

ABOUT THE AUTHOR

I'm a romantic suspense writer fueled by Dr. Pepper and chocolate. Part-time chef, full-time weather nerd, and mom to both 2-legged and 4-legged children. My journey into the world of romance and suspense started when my grandma handed me her well-worn copies of Danielle Steel and Nora Roberts novels—I was hooked.

During the Covid lockdowns, with time on my hands and a need for catharsis, I dove into writing my own romantic suspense novels. Fast forward several years and four novels later, I'm ready to share my stories with the world. My books are a thrilling blend of romance, mystery, and suspense —think *Cupid Meets Crime Scene*.

www.AllisonBettes.com

facebook.com/AuthorAllisonBettes

instagram.com/authorallisonbettes

tiktok.com/@allison.bettes